The Weaver

and the Factory Maid

Also by Deborah Grabien

Plainsong
Eyes in the Fire

The **Weaver**

and the **Factory Maid**

Deborah Grabien

THOMAS DUNNE BOOKS / ST. MARTIN'S MINOTAUR ≈ NEW YORK

THOMAS DUNNE BOOKS.
An imprint of St. Martin's Press.

www.minotaurbooks.com

Library of Congress Cataloging-in-Publication Data

Grabien, Deborah.
    The weaver and the factory maid / Deborah Grabien.—1st ed.
     p. cm.
    ISBN 0-312-31422-1
    1. Folk musicians—Fiction. 2. Padstow (England)—Fiction.
  3. Historic buildings—Fiction. 4. Murder victims—Fiction.
  5. Haunted houses—Fiction. 6. Ballads—Fiction. I. Title.

PS3557.R1145W43 2003
813'.54—dc21

                         2003050618

First Edition: December 2003

10 9 8 7 6 5 4 3 2 1

For the musicians of the UK folk world

Acknowledgments

Some thanks and acknowledgments are due, not only for this novel, but for all the stories that I hope will follow.

Tad Williams and Deb Beale, for feeding and soothing while we researched in the UK.

My beloved anarachs, with special thanks to Betsy Hanes Perry.

Jennifer Jackson, excellent agent, and everyone at DMLA.

Nic, of course.

Marlene Shannon-Stringer, for hand-holding, painfully deep edits, moral support, and taking time away from her own writing to perform the tender mercies listed above.

And Ruth Cavin, who took the book, shook it upside down, got all the nasty fuzzy bits off it, and made it the book it is now.

The Weaver
and the Factory Maid

One

Unite and unite and let us all unite
For summer is a-coming today.

—from "Padstow Mayday"

On a bright Saturday afternoon in Cornwall, the Padstow Mayday Celebration was in full swing.

The musical part of the annual festivities had begun the previous afternoon. Musicians, many of whom hadn't met since last year's event, swapped arrangements, slandered their record companies, or gossiped. Costumed morris dancers entertained the crowd, who danced through the streets after the brightly painted Hobby Horse. The weather was warm, soft, and breezy. There was also beer, cheap and plentiful. An all-around sense of contentment pervaded the air.

Still, nothing's perfect. Three musicians, members of the Broomfield Hill Quartet, were not enjoying themselves as much as they would have liked.

"Hasn't anyone heard from Ringan?"

Jane Castle's famous three-octave voice was sounding shrill. Since the tiny singer was as well known for her serenity as she was for her vocal range, her two companions were taking notice.

"I've told you twice, love, not since yesterday." Liam McCall, six feet five and rail-thin, flitted around the dusty room in Padstow's Institute like a nervous moth, picking up his fiddle and setting it down again. As if punctuating his reply to Jane, he took up the instrument and plucked a few notes, banjo style. He then glared at it, muttered, "American hillbilly tunes, oh hell," and put it back in its case.

"Oh, leave the damned fiddle alone, can't you?" Liam's restlessness seemed to irritate Jane past endurance. "For heaven's sake, Liam, must you putter?"

"I like to putter." He looked at Jane. "Shall I say it again, then? Four times lucky, maybe? He rang up to say there was a problem with this house he's been working on, and could we swap times with one of the other groups, and he'd be here this evening. All right? Got it all clear now?"

"So we've swapped with Martin and Dave. I know that." If anything, Jane's voice had gone a bit higher. She said peevishly, "Why does he want to muck about with other people's houses in the middle of the bloody Festival, anyway?"

"Because he doesn't fancy starving for his art." Liam's restless eye lit on a half-full pint glass of the local ale, abandoned by someone else hours earlier. He grabbed it, gulped, and winced. As the others watched, he muttered, "Flat as a pancake and not mine anyway, sorry," and set it down. Wiping his mouth with the back of one hand, he added in a fair-minded way, "Can't blame him, can you?"

"I bloody well can blame him!" Since Jane knew that playing traditional music in the modern world was a highly unreliable method of bill-paying, this was unfair. Liam opened his mouth to blister her, but was forestalled.

"He'll get here. When has Ringan ever missed a gig?" Matty Curran offered a sleepy smile. "Stop fretting, Jane. It'll be fine. It's not as if he's got far to come."

"I forgot, he's not in London." She looked relieved. Matty Curran had that effect on people. "Near Glastonbury, isn't he? Only a few hours' driving."

"Less than that, the way Ringan drives." Matty, large and placid, rested his heels on his accordion case. "And Martin said he and Dave would be glad to switch set times with us. So we don't go on until half nine tonight. Dave said something about an arrangement of 'Padstow Mayday' they want to try. Nice of them, all things considered."

"Opportunistic of them, all things considered."

"Beg pardon?"

"Well, it's Mayday, isn't it? And we're in Padstow. And, as I recall, they've got a new CD to promote." Jane let her breath out. "Sorry. I didn't mean to go all hysterical at you. I'm sure Ringan will get here in plenty of time."

"Too right he will." Liam grabbed his violin and moved toward the door. "Bright-eyed and bushy-tailed and with the grand guitar Lord Randall in hand. Let's go down the pub while it's still licensing hours. Jane can buy me a pint."

The others followed, Jane pausing long enough to ask, "Why me?"

"Why not?" Liam said simply, and headed for the street.

At about the time that Liam was juggling three pint glasses toward a table in a Padstow pub, Rupert Darnley Laine, known as Ringan, was facing the Right Honourable Albert Wychsale, the man who had hired him to help renovate the family's Somerset manor. Albert Wychsale, the current Baron Boult, had just given Ringan a piece of very unwelcome news. And Ringan was not taking it well at all.

"What do you mean, you can't pay me?"

Ringan's voice, which held strong overtones of a Scots burr, was downright warlike. It reminded Wychsale of things like Macbeth and the Glencoe massacre. And surely the study was no place for blue jeans or for a shabby guitar case with "C. F. Martin & Co." stencilled on it. In the serene room, a pugnacious Scots musician was a disharmonious element.

The backdrop for this tension was charming. The study was a large, airy room, set like a jewel in Wychsale House, a gracious Queen Anne manor between Baltonsborough and Glastonbury. The study was sunlit and welcoming. Enter, it seemed to say, and sit in one of these exquisite wing chairs designed by George Hepplewhite. Drink a brandy, cross your legs, admire the vistas across the terrace and landscaped gardens. Listen to the distant murmur of the River Brue or of its tributary, the Carlyon. Rest, or remember past glories, or dream of fishing and England and a good long nap. It was a dignified room, mellowed with time, poorly suited for tension; which, at the moment, was what it was getting.

Albert Wychsale cleared his throat unhappily. "I'm afraid you misunderstood me."

"Oh, did I, now."

The Scots burr seemed to thicken as Ringan got angrier. Wychsale, sixtyish and a bit on the portly side, abandoned thoughts of Glencoe and envisioned instead little naked blue-painted savages, lunching on their enemies. He picked his words very carefully. "I didn't say I couldn't pay you for your work, Mr. Laine. I merely said I couldn't pay you in cash at this point in time."

Ringan's jaw, thrust forward so that his black beard jutted at a dangerous angle, did not relax. Despite the fact that he was actually smaller than his erstwhile employer, he somehow looked larger. "That sounds like a statement of nonpayment to me. We signed a contract, remember? Before I sank three months of my time, plus expenses, into restoring your property."

"Mr. Laine, if you would just—"

Ringan cut him off, waving a hand toward the surface of the writing table that suddenly seemed, in Wychsale's eyes, a very flimsy barrier between them. "A copy of the invoice is on your desk. It's completely itemized. You signed off on it yesterday. You owe me seventy-eight hundred quid."

"Yes, yes, I know that." Wychsale mopped his brow. He didn't know what upset him more, the confrontation with the angry Scot or the Scot's evident belief that Wychsale meant to cheat him. "Let me assure you, Mr. Laine, I have every intention of paying you. I can pay you this moment if you'd like; in fact, I was going to suggest a way to do it, but the situation is a bit odd. There's a comfortable chair behind you. If you'd just sit down and let me explain?"

4

"I know there's a chair. I found the chairs and ordered them for you, remember? And I'll stand, thank you."

"Certainly. Whatever you choose." Wychsale took a deep breath and plunged in headlong. "In a nutshell, the problem is this. Three days ago, I asked my broker to liquidate the shares I hold in a well-known North Sea energy consortium. For cash-flow purposes."

Ringan wasn't giving an inch. "So?"

"So, I heard from my broker this morning. He informed me that the company whose shares I was planning to sell has gone into bankruptcy. It's been seized by the government, and all assets frozen. I'm assuming you haven't seen the financial news today." Wychsale hated being forced to explain; fifteen generations of landed English gentry had gone into making him. Landed gentry didn't usually have to explain to the hired help. "And since I have three other loans out, all of which I'd been securing with those shares, my liquid cash just vanished into limbo until this mess gets sorted out. The sorting-out could take months. This isn't just big-money interests, either. It's going to have a ripple effect that hits everything in the financial world and beyond. This is a big one, Mr. Laine, a catastrophic crash of a huge company. And it honestly isn't my fault. No one seems to have seen it coming, not even the board of directors."

There was a long silence. Wychsale, who had been looking everywhere except at Ringan, glanced up and made a discovery. Ringan no longer looked militant. He looked worried. In fact, he looked so worried that Wychsale asked a stupid question. "Is something the matter, Mr. Laine?"

"You said an energy consortium. A North Sea energy consortium." Ringan sounded worried, too. "Do me a huge favour and tell me it isn't the Three Towers syndicate."

"I could tell you that," Wychsale said. "But I'd be lying. Three Towers it is."

Ringan looked around him, discovered one of the Hepplewhite chairs, and sank into it as though his legs had stopped working. The black beard was limp; the flesh around his mouth had gone an unhealthy blue-white.

"Mr. Laine?" Wychsale, at heart a decent man, forgot his nervousness and came around the writing table. "Good heavens, are you all right?"

"Oh, I'm fine," Ringan said bitterly. "I'm just too wonderful for words. My mother won't be, though. Most of her income, about ninety percent of it in fact, comes from her shares in that bloody company. Which means that I'm going to have to cough up a nice bit of my already paltry income to help her out. Damn, damn, bloody double sweating damn!"

"Oh, dear." Beneath his genuine concern, Wychsale felt a flicker of relief. This little development might just make Laine more amenable to the admittedly peculiar solution Wychsale was planning to propose. "I'm so sorry. If it's any consolation, quite a lot of people are probably feeling pretty sick right now."

"I'm sure they are. But I'm not consoled." Ringan met his eyes and said sourly, "All right, Mr. Wychsale. I'm obviously over a barrel, so let's put the cards on the table. You mentioned a suggestion for paying me right now. Let's hear it."

"Of course, of course." The battle, Wychsale thought, was pretty well won. "As I said, I can't pay you in cold cash. And since Wychsale House is entailed, tied property, I'm forbidden to sell any of it to raise money. But there is one thing I could do. You told me that you live in a rented flat in London. What I have in mind is simply this . . ."

He proceeded to explain. With every word, Ringan Laine felt a bit better.

Ringan made it from Wychsale House to Padstow in two and a half hours.

It was lucky for him that he drove as well as he did. His car, a ten-year-old Alfa Romeo in perfect condition, darted through city traffic without any conscious thought on its driver's part. It ate up the miles on the M5 like a greedy child with a bag of sweets. And if the police were about on this beautiful Saturday, they remained decently invisible, which, had Ringan thought about it, was lucky. He was in no condition to offer explanations or apologies.

The scenery, some of it lovely, passed by in a blur. Ringan's driving skills and sense of location were on total automatic pilot. His brain was otherwise occupied.

Boiled down to basics, Wychsale's solution to the problem was breathtaking in its simplicity. Ringan needed payment; Wychsale's financial liquidity had just solidified with the speed of cold water in a deep freeze. Therefore, two options remained: payment in cash, which might take months to achieve, or payment in property. Ringan turned onto the motorway, let the clutch in, changed up to a higher gear, and thought back to bits of the conversation.

"But you've told me . . . I studied the records . . . the Wychsale demesne, in fact all the Boult ancestral holdings, are tied property . . . you can't dispose of any of it . . . are you talking about personal property, a painting or something?"

"Not personal property . . . the entailment only applies to the original demesne . . . there's one bit, about an acre and a half of land . . . a small cottage and a reconstructed tithe barn . . . purchased by my family at the beginning of the nineteenth century . . . mine to use in any way I see fit."

The Alfa cut between two slower vehicles, accelerated smoothly, and jumped forward into the fast lane. Ringan didn't hear the blare of irritated car horns behind him. It was twenty past four in the afternoon, and he had to be in Padstow in time to hook up with Jane and Matty and Liam. It occurred to him that he didn't have a clue as to what time he was supposed to be performing, or what, or where. Maybe he'd already missed this gig; maybe the band had already gone on without him. If that was the case, Jane at least was going to have a few words for him, and maybe an antique Gemeinhardt flute to the back of his skull. He shrugged off the notion and thought back to Wychsale's astonishing, elegant solution. The conversation, muddled by Ringan's own reaction to Wychsale's bombshell, grew clearer in his mind.

"You're suggesting payment in property . . . a lifetime leasehold on a

parcel of land on the Carlyon River . . . a small cottage . . . an old barn."

"Exactly. You'd be responsible for the county taxes . . . minimal . . . already checked with my solicitor. Far less than you pay for one month on a London flat . . . already paid this year's, anyway . . . you'd own it, at least for your lifetime. It would revert to the Wychsale estate at your, um, demise."

The Alfa, travelling well over the posted limits, had left Somerset behind. Ringan had cut over to the A30 without even thinking. He'd crossed over the River Tamar and gotten well into Cornwall. Road signs with the names of towns flashed by: Lewdown, Tinhay, Bolventor. One corner of his eye caught the sign he wanted: Bodmin, and the distance remaining to reach it.

"But that land must be worth a fortune. And a cottage with it? You're talking about settling a debt of just under eight thousand pounds with something worth many times that much. Why? It doesn't make sense."

"Actually, it does. You see, I'd have to sell that bit anyway. That could take months, with the economy in its current state. There are other considerations, as well . . ."

Ringan changed lanes, made the cut, and headed for the western coast.

The two hemispheres of his brain wrestled madly with each other. The left side was picking through the various legal aspects of suddenly becoming a member of the moneyed classes, trying to correlate costs of renovating the cottage, weighing the positive aspects of moving from London to Somerset against the negatives. The right side of his brain was a confused mess, stupefied with conflicting feelings, and it couldn't cope; there was simply too much input, too much to deal with at once. He wanted to stop the Alfa, find a phone, ring his mother in Scotland, and find out how that very odd woman was taking the news of her financial disaster. He wanted to ring his girlfriend, whose theatre troupe was playing a two-week engagement near York. He wanted to call his brother Duncan and his sister Roberta and let them in on the news.

Mostly, though, he wanted to turn the car around and take it straight back to Somerset. Hell, he thought, I'd like to blow off the

Festival, get back to the little cottage on the banks of the Carlyon, walk all through it and tell myself, over and over, that it's now mine. Of such small moments is heaven made on earth. Surely he was entitled to one occasionally.

". . . proximity between the cottage and the main house is another consideration. I wouldn't like to sell to someone I might not find, um, congenial as a neighbor. A stranger might have dogs, or small children. I'm not fond of either, I'm afraid. But we've worked closely for the past few months. By and large, you're a nice, even-tempered chap. I'm sure you'd be a fine neighbor. Let me show you around the place. That way you'd get a better idea as to whether you liked it . . ."

Ringan glanced at his watch. Nearly six, with another twenty minutes of driving to do. He'd dump the Alfa in a carpark and head straight for the Institute. If the others weren't there, someone would know where to find them. It ought to be simple enough. Knowing Liam, the nearest pub would do nicely. After all, the pubs opened again at six . . .

"Here we go. Lumbe's started out as a laborer's cottage, ground floor only. The first floor—two small bedrooms and a bath—were added later, on two separate occasions. For such a little place, Lumbe's Cottage has quite a history . . ."

Ringan pulled up to the outskirts of Padstow, nosed the Alfa into the first space he saw, and climbed out. For a moment he stood, his beloved guitar, Lord Randall, dangling from one hand, and surveyed one of the loveliest sunsets in Britain. The sky was showing the night fires of Mayday, lighting up everything from the Abbey House on the North Quay to the mouth of the Camel Estuary. The distant hush and sough of the waves carried the singing of the town's celebrants in the distance. It was a charming picture.

Ringan sighed, a soft acknowledgment of relaxation. He had just made the decision to abandon London for the West Country with remarkably little fuss. All he wanted to do now was to get into town, locate whichever pub the other members of the Broomfield Hill Quartet were presently drinking in, and share in the good news.

9

"Right," said Ringan, and headed down the hill toward Padstow at a fast trot.

At ten, the Institute was packed with an enthusiastic but well-behaved crowd. They were cheering the efforts of an Irish harpist who specialized in playing compositions by the legendary blind harpist Turlough O'Carolan, as Broomfield Hill tuned up their instruments offstage.

Whether because of Ringan's safe arrival, or simply because she was so comfortable performing, Jane had regained her usual serenity. Apart from meting out a mild scold at being given such a fright, she displayed none of her earlier waspishness. Upon Ringan's entrance into the pub where they'd been relaxing, Matty had bought him a pint and told him to drink up. He'd also hushed Liam's boisterous demands to know what in hell Ringan thought he'd been up to, telling the fiddler sternly to let the poor bloke drink in peace. Between long mouthfuls of the local brew, Ringan had obliged with the entire story. Their dropped jaws, in his opinion, had been very gratifying.

Later, in the wings at the Padstow Institute, Liam returned to the subject. He'd dealt with his own instrument, and waited for Ringan to adjust the tuning pegs on Lord Randall before asking his question.

"So what d'you suppose the catch is, then?"

"I've been asking myself that same thing all day." Ringan, who had tuned both E strings down to D, remembered that their first piece was in concert tuning, and patiently adjusted his strings back to normal. Liam's question echoed his own main concern. "One thing's sure," he went on, keeping an ear on the guitar's harmonics. "If I find a single bloody loophole that doesn't go in my favour, the deal's off. I don't care if the Right Hon's got to sell his poor pitiful aged mum to the gypsies, he tries to put one over on me and he pays in cash."

"Has he got an aged mum?"

Jane, her flute lying in her lap, put the question in all seriousness.

Matty gave her his gentle smile, and she smiled back. So did Ringan. "If he does, she's packed away in mothballs somewhere," he said.

The Irish harpist, having finished her second encore, came off stage to thunderous applause, and nodded to Ringan. He stood and picked up Lord Randall. "That's our cue. On we go, then."

Considering the day's distractions, Broomfield Hill played an excellent set. They opened with an a cappella version of "Reynardine," a piece designed to show off Jane's staggering voice. As the first pure, icy notes soared over the room, half the audience mouthed along with her: *One morning as I rambled along the leaves so green, I overheard a young woman converse with Reynardine . . .*

They followed with an instrumental medley of Irish tunes. The crowd now nicely warmed up, Broomfield Hill gratified them with a group of traditional standards: "Henry Martin," "The Banks of Yarrow," "Black Waterside," and a hilariously bawdy bit called "The Bonny Black Hare," sung by Matty and Ringan while Jane relaxed with a tambourine and Liam fiddled as if he thought Rome might start burning without him. They worked their way through a quarter hour of instrumental music, including a few reels and a hauntingly delicate flute solo that Jane had composed some months earlier. They ended the set with Jane's and Ringan's dueling vocals on "Bruton Town" and offered the deliriously approving audience— who understood that this was the end of the day's music—an encore of their signature tune, "Broomfield Hill." With a hearty good night and a recommendation to find their way home safely, the band left the stage and the house lights came up. Thus ended the Padstow Mayday, and one of the oddest days Ringan Laine had ever spent.

Two

I am a hand-weaver to my trade
I fell in love with a factory maid,
And if I could but her favour win,
I'd stand beside her and weave by steam.

A month after his conversation with Albert Wychsale, Ringan unlocked the front door of Lumbe's Cottage and officially took possession of his new home.

He'd bid farewell to London without regret. Growing up in the Scottish Highlands, Ringan had spent his childhood running barefoot in the hills with his sister and brother. He'd grown familiar with the smell of heather, and he'd cursed the gorse when it scratched him. He'd learned how to ride a pony, and how to tell one species of migrating bird from another. He'd also accumulated a vast store of traditional Scottish songs. In those days, Glasgow had seemed as vast a metropolis as ancient Rome.

His university years, followed by the burgeoning sprawl of Britain's folk music scene, had changed all that. Gaining a reputation as a world-class guitarist, Ringan had gone where the music scene of the eighties and nineties had taken him; Glasgow to Liverpool to London, with all points along the way. An American tour had put the seal on his personal urbanisation. No one can spend time in the streets of New York and Los Angeles and remain a rustic. He'd long ago come to consider himself a city-dweller.

Now, as if the vibrant smell of freshly-turned soil and the mysterious rustlings of haystack and hedgerow had lain dormant in him all along, he made an interesting discovery: he loathed city life.

Apparently, he was still a country boy at heart, and had been, all along.

So, on a golden summer day, Ringan set his hand-grip and Lord Randall's case on the floor of the tiny entrance hall, and took a moment to convince himself that this odd, idyllic little place was his own.

Lumbe's Cottage was a patchwork of styles and additions, cobbled together over two centuries. Ringan had learned something of its history from Albert Wychsale, and slightly more from a fast look at the records in Wychsale House's Muniment Room. The original one-room shack had been built in 1790, to house a family of seven labourers. In those days, of course, labourers were considered as common as tea, and far cheaper to buy. The working classes under King George III could hardly afford to be choosy, not when anyone with a few acres and any social standing at all could own them, body and soul, for a paltry two pounds a year. The idea brought Ringan's hackles upright; people as a commodity, cheaper than tea? Seven people in one room, with no plumbing? Horrible.

Ringan stepped into what had once comprised that unknown family's living space and surveyed it. While it must have been cramped for a family, the room's eighteen by twenty-four feet was perfect for a single man. It had once been a rectangle. Now, thanks to such additions as an upper floor and a scullery, the rectangle had been broken in several interesting ways.

The north wall still boasted the original fireplace that had been the centre of the cottage's excuse for a kitchen in King George's day. The surrounding walls were brick, mellowed with long use to a fine patina. The floor, which Ringan guessed had been mere packed earth at the time of construction, had been covered with parquet. Victorian, he thought, mid-nineteenth century, done about the time that Dickens's pen was in full flow. The ceilings were pitched low, barely seven feet, and the lintels lower still. Ringan thought, grinning, that Liam would spend his visits ducking and swearing. The leaded windows let the sun in, casting dancing patterns of bright colour across the wood.

He walked the length of the room, savoring it, hearing the soft voice of the Carlyon flowing by at the end of his garden path. He glanced at the door opposite the fireplace, which led to the present-day kitchen, primitive by current standards but adequate for him. According to Wychsale, it had been installed as a scullery during the Boer War, then expanded and updated to meet both the severe housing shortage and the electrical requirements of World War II's early years. It had two tiny windows, and an herb garden outside its Dutch doors. At the moment, it held Ringan's answering machine and telephone, as well as a dozen cardboard cartons containing his immediate necessities, stacked in two tidy piles against the wall where a small table might eventually sit.

One thing was certain. He might be one of Britain's foremost experts on the restoration of period architecture, but this time, he was off the hook. There was no point in bringing the cottage back to its original state. You'd want to be a fanatic, not a historian, to do something that stupid. It was far nicer and more livable as it was now.

Beside the kitchen wall was a flight of stairs. Ringan, instinctively and unnecessarily ducking his head, made his way up toward the first floor, where bedrooms and a bath had been added. Sunlight splashed across the wooden risers, dappling Ringan's jeans and tennis shoes with colour.

The stairs bent halfway up, forming a small landing, where someone had added a lovely round window. Since it seemed to be the stairwell's only source of light, getting around at night might prove bothersome. He thought about bumped heads and twisted ankles, made a mental note to ask his landlord about wiring, and remembered that the landlord in question was himself. He grinned, a bit ruefully. This "it's your problem, mate, you fix it" business would take some getting used to . . .

He turned the bend in the stairs, headed for the first floor, and stopped as if he'd been hit with a bullet.

The shaft of cold, as icy as it was unexpected, stabbed him between the shoulder blades. He was standing in a pool of sunlight, the temperature was over seventy, and he'd just been thinking about opening some windows to cool the place off. Yet, for one incredulous moment, he'd felt as if he'd walked into an ice box. Every hair on his body bristled, and his knees went rubbery. And he suddenly wanted to burst into tears. The shock was enormous. What in hell . . . ?

The cold faded as quickly as it had come, easing in the blink of an eye to a soft rush of cool air before dying away. There was, there seemed to be, a soft touch against him, the brush of something: breath, fabric, fingertips? He didn't know; it was too indistinct, and gone too soon. For a moment Ringan thought he'd heard a sigh behind him.

With trembling legs and erratic heartbeat, he put out a sweaty hand and leaned weakly against the wall. It was warm under his palm. That chilly blast had not come from the open space between the stairs and the kitchen.

He was breathing deeply, wondering where the icy breath had come from and why it had left him wanting to cry, when a car pulled up on the lawn outside. Ringan heard the engine die, and the sharp slam of a car door. He shivered, pulled himself together, and walked down the stairs in time to hear his name called in a deep, lovely contralto.

"Ringan? Are you here?"

Penelope Wintercraft-Hawkes, looking like a Uccello noble-woman gone gloriously decadent, poked her head through the front door. Ringan, silently commanding his knees to stop trembling, came down to meet her.

"In the flesh, for what it's worth." He was, in a remote fashion, amazed at how normal he sounded. "Hullo, Penny, my only love. You can't think how glad I am to see you. Come in, come in. Mind you don't trip over Lord Randall. What on earth are you doing here? Did you drive all the way down from York to congratulate the new homeowner?"

"No, darling, only from Bath. I've been visiting with Richard and Candy." She dropped her overnight bag on the floor, stepping around the guitar case and into Ringan's arms. "Ringan," she said happily. "Ringan Ringan Ringan. Have you ever told me why you're Ringan and not Rupert?"

"Wouldn't you be, if your mum was daft enough to name you Rupert? You've never asked. It's just an old nickname, is all; very Scots." He wrapped both arms around her. "Hullo, lamb. How are you, and Richard and Candy, and all? And really, what brings you down?"

For a few seconds, locked together, it would have been difficult to tell them apart. They were much of a height and of a remarkably similar physical type: Ringan's average height and finely-boned strong build translated, in his lady, to a willowy effect of leg and muscle. Both were black-haired, and they each had the kind of mobility to their features that bespoke agility of body and mind alike.

"Fine, thanks. They send congratulations and greetings, and a jar of honey as a house-gift." Penny kissed him, full on the lips. "Hullo back to you, bearded boy. What am I doing here? Well, we wrapped up the engagement in York three days ago. Nice reviews from the press. Do you know, I think some of them might even have read Thomas Kyd before they reviewed the production? Well, no, maybe not."

"Ah. The *Spanish Tragedy,* wasn't it? I think you're rating the literacy of the British press too high. What makes you think they can read at all?"

"My good-hearted naivete, that's what. My overwhelming desire to believe the best of people." She kissed him again, and snaked one hand around the back of his head. Her wide mouth was relaxed and happy. "Ooh, you're all clammy. And you were looking a bit green when I came in, but now you're not. Ringan, what a glorious little house this is. Utterly picture-postcard, all E. M. Forster and Beatrix Potter, by way of Merchant-Ivory. The ivy climbing all over the walls is almost too much. Was that an herb garden I spotted, round the side?"

"Probably. I haven't explored the gardens much; in fact, I've only just started exploring the house." He dropped his arm around her waist and thought about how gorgeous she was. Wild black hair, razor-sharp cheekbones, legs up to her neck. Maybe it was a good thing they didn't live together; seeing her was a fresh delight every time. "I was working most of May myself, remember? Touring with the band in Scotland."

"Did you get a chance to see your mum?"

"I did." Ringan shuddered at the memory. Maggie Laine, theatrically patriotic and genuinely eccentric, was tricky enough to cope with under normal circumstances. This time, he'd found her draped in black like an Edwardian stage dowager, figuratively wringing her hands and literally bemoaning the cruelty of fate, which had stripped her of her worldly goods and made her dependent upon the whims of her uncaring children. Since all three of her uncaring children were in attendance, arranging with great inconvenience to themselves and without complaint for bits of their income to be made over for her support, these theatrics had been as inaccurate as they were unfair. Duncan and Ringan had held on to their tempers with difficulty. Their sister Roberta hadn't been quite so forbearing. Things had nearly got out of hand.

Still, the problem had been taken care of. All Ringan wanted to do now was to forget about it. "So how is the Mann Clan these days, anyway?" he asked.

Penny accepted the tacit change of subject. She and Ringan had been lovers for ten years, and she could read every twitch of his mouth or lift of his eyebrows. She liked to tell people who asked her why they didn't get married, or at least try living together, that cohabitation was a device invented by hungry divorce lawyers. As for marriage, no one in their right mind would add a Penny Laine to a family that already boasted a Candy Mann.

"They're fine. Richard was actually at home for a change. He'd just finished producing something for American telly." Penny shivered with distaste; she was a rarity, a theatrical producer with a pathological dislike of cameras. "And Candy has taken up bee-keeping, of all things."

"Ah, that explains it. I was wondering why they'd send a jar of honey. Beekeeping, though; isn't that a bit risky?" They had stepped into the main room; Penny was prowling its length, smiling and entranced. "I thought your little sister was allergic to insect venom?"

"Not allergic, just terrified. She says she decided that this would be a good way to confront it. Too Freudian and new-age of her. I adore her, you know that, but I honestly think she's got Sainsbury's tinned peas where her brains ought to be. I mean, wouldn't you think spraying herself with Bug-Be-Gone or something would be more sensible?" She pushed open the kitchen door and danced through it. "Ringan, this place is exquisite! How old is it? Who put the new cooker in here? And what were you planning to do about furniture?"

Ringan's jaw dropped. "So that's why the rooms looked so huge! I've only just realised there's no furniture. Oh, Lord, my brains must be as unreliable as Candy's. Is there a new cooker in there? There wasn't when I made it down last week to get the phone installation seen to."

"Dear old British Telcom. Their splendors are varied, and wondrous to behold. Maybe your noble patron had the cooker installed. Quite nice of him, really. But it's going to be a bloody nuisance trying to get beds up those stairs." Her voice sounded distant; she had unlatched the kitchen's Dutch doors and moved into the garden. "I'm assuming the upstairs is unfurnished as well. Darling, what a marvelous garden! Look, there's rosemary and comfrey, and I think that fuzzy plant over there is a variety of mint . . ."

"I told you, I haven't seen the gardens. I haven't been upstairs, either. You arrived just as I was going up." Something in his voice must have caught her attention, for she turned and stared at him, her brows drawn together. He cursed silently; it wouldn't do to forget how acute she was. He said smoothly, "You're right, that's a new cooker. Gas, too; cheap to run. I must remember to thank Wychsale."

He came out, noting the enraptured tilt to Penny's head as she squatted among the herbs. As he knelt beside her, she pulled a leaf free of its stem and handed it to him. A fragrant smell clung to his fingers.

"Mint it is," Ringan said appreciatively. "This garden is quite nice. How long can you stay, love?"

Penny's dark eyes were dreamy. "Three full weeks, do you believe it? Then it's off to Surrey for two weeks' rehearsal, and a month at the Copenhagen Arts Festival. I've got the troupe doing Marlowe."

"Really, Madame Producer, how twee." Ringan rubbed the sprig of mint between his fingers. "Are your Tamburlaine Players honestly tacky enough to inflict *Tamburlaine* Part I on all those poor bewildered Danes?"

"Don't be cheeky." She offered him an enchanting grin. "We're doing *Faustus*. Speaking of twee, what's that blocky-looking building over there, with the thatched roof? Is it yours as well?"

"It's a reconstructed tithe barn, and yes, it's mine. I haven't gone inside yet. I'd thought about using it as a working space, for Broomfield Hill. That's assuming it's suitable, of course. For all I know, that picturesque roof over there may leak like a sieve."

"No problem. If you keep Liam drunk enough, he won't mind the drips." Penny got up and brushed the loamy soil from the knees of her trousers. "Did I hear you say you haven't been upstairs yet? Let's go explore."

For a moment, Ringan felt an odd reluctance. As Penny headed through the Dutch door, pausing to watch him with one eyebrow raised, he remembered the cold, the sensation of breath against, his own weakness. It was a memory as visceral as anything he'd ever experienced. Cold, very cold, a nasty sharp bitter blast of pure cold. Cold like an arrow in an empty house, cold on a summer's day, cold that sucked the strength from your legs and made you want to weep . . .

"Ringan? Hello? Are you expected back soon, by any chance?"

He jerked his head, focussed on Penny, and managed a smile. "Sorry. I'd toddled off to Mars there for a moment. As you said, let's go explore."

Back in the kitchen, Ringan subjected the room to a quick inventory. The new cooker—he must call Wychsale and thank him—and a small fridge, much older. A Welsh dresser, too big for the room to be aesthetically pleasing; still, since it seemed to be the only cupboard space on the ground floor, quite useful. Big old-fashioned copper sink. Pseudo-brick floor tiles, dating back to the Jazz Age by the look of them. Electrical outlets scanty, but adequate for his needs. And, next to the inside door, another door. Something that was obviously an under-the-stairs storage space.

"Good Lord, don't look so worried. What do you suppose is in there? The family skeleton?"

Ringan jumped violently at the sound of her voice. For a moment he'd forgotten her presence. "I'm damned if I know. Shall we find out?"

"If it will explain why you're so bloody jumpy, yes."

She sounded tart. It was ridiculous that anyone should be able to read his moods like that, and intolerable that she should believe he was frightened. The thought stiffened him; squaring his shoulders, he popped the slip-latch free and swung the door open.

"Ah." Penny peered over his shoulder. "Mystery solved, ghost laid. How old do you suppose that water heater is, anyway? It looks to be in excellent shape, but . . ."

"Forty years, at least. The place hasn't been lived in since the Second World War, so it hasn't seen much wear and tear on the pipes. Come along, love, let's go upstairs and see the sights." Not a whisper of that disturbing cold; nothing but a water heater. Relief made him giddy. He shut the door, refastened the latch, and led the way upstairs.

They had reached the first floor before Ringan realised that he'd been expecting another blast of cold. It didn't come; all he felt was the warm June air. He was so relieved that he reached out and took Penny's hand, pulling her against him and kissing her hard and fast on the lips as she came up behind him.

"Mmm," she said when she'd caught her breath, "very nice, very nice indeed. What was that in aid of?"

"Sheer self-indulgence. What shall we look at first? There's a master bedroom, a small bedroom, and a full bath."

"The bathroom," she said at once. "But you'll have to wait to look until after I use it."

"No toilet paper, or probably not."

"Not to worry." She fumbled in her pockets and pulled out a fistful of tissues. "I believe in being prepared for any eventuality. Comes from touring in the provinces, not to mention on the Continent. Back in a tick."

She disappeared through the bathroom door, only to poke her head out immediately. "Ringan, you've got to see this!"

The bathroom was not an inch larger than it needed to be. Its shuttered windows faced the river, its floor was Italian marble, and its sink was perfect Edwardian. There was even a lavabo, made of fine china and flowered round the edges. But the prize was the bath, a vast, claw-footed monster straight out of a Victorian gentleman's magazine.

Penny regarded it with awe. "Do you know," she said, "I honestly think we could both fit into that thing and take a bath at the same time, and never even have to say hello to each other? Have you ever seen anything so huge?"

"Yes, at your parents' house. Why do you think I asked you to marry me, the first time I stayed at Whistler's Croft? I'd seen the upstairs guest bath, that's why, and I wanted to make sure I'd inherit it." He ran a hand lovingly over the porcelain surface. "By Christ, what a beauty! Look at those dragon's-head taps! Polished brass, no less. You can't buy one of these today at any price. Even if I have to spend money on furniture, the tub makes it worth it. May heaven bless my—what did you call him? My noble patron?"

"No shower," she pointed out, in a fair-minded spirit.

"I don't give a damn. Why bother with showers when I can waste a week's supply of hot water by filling a tub this size? Why are you pushing at me like that?"

"Because if I don't pee I'll burst, that's why. Go on, get out."

While she was busy, Ringan took the opportunity to open the door to the smaller bedroom. His exclamation of delight coincided with Penny's emergence from the loo. She came and peered over his shoulder.

"Oh, how lovely!"

This room, at least, had been furnished. The walls were covered by a delicately flocked paper, and the polished wooden floor boasted a braided rug that would have brought a tidy sum at any antique shop. Ringan, who knew quite a lot about period furniture, stood in stunned silence; there was a walnut chiffonier, a full-sized cheval glass in a swinging frame, a marble-topped vanity, and a beautiful tester bed that sat elegantly beneath the dormer window. Every stick of furniture in the room was at least a hundred years old, and none of it had been cheap when new. For a moment it took his breath away.

"Bloody hell," he said, finding his voice. "I'd say this calls for a nice bottle of wine for my noble patron. He's certainly done me proud."

"Ringan," Penny said, her brows furrowed, "there must be five thousand quid worth of stuff in this room alone. How much did you say this bloke up at the manor house owed you?"

"Seventy-eight hundred, to be exact."

"Then I simply don't understand. Has he gone out of his mind? Is he trying to hide this from his other creditors? Or—or what?"

Ringan ran a finger over the marble surface of the table. It came up coated with dust. "I think he forgot this stuff was here. True, there's a Sotheby's auction in this room alone. But you must remember, O pampered daughter of the upper classes, that compared to what he's got up at Wychsale House, this lot's nothing. I ordered a set of eight chairs and a table for the dining room that cost about three times what this whole room would fetch. Oh!" He suddenly let loose with a short bark of laughter. "I'm a twit, that's what. Of course, that's it!"

"What's it?" There was a peculiar look on Penny's face; her head was tilted and her neck stretched, as if she were trying to hear some faraway voice. "Ringan . . ."

"That's why he was so bloody anxious for me to accept this place! Don't you see, love? All of his other creditors were nice, genteel businesses that would wait the six months to get paid. They wouldn't be in any hurry to incur the wrath of the Right Honourable." Despite himself, Ringan was grinning; the idea of having brought the aristocracy to its financial knees was too funny to be offensive. "The only one he couldn't trust not to raise hell, and maybe file a lien against his estate, was the uppity peasant from the North Country. And, of course, if I went and filed a lien, the others would shrug their well-bred shoulders and make noises of regret and start filing as well. Up the revolution! Come on, let's see what the master bedroom's got to show."

He darted across the hall, Penny following slowly. She stopped once, looking dizzy and confused. Then, shaking her head like a swimmer coming out of deep water, she joined him in the larger bedroom. He was openly gloating.

"Look at it! Turkey carpet, standing wardrobe with rosewood inlays, and that bed! Personally, I'd say this lot was a princely bribe to placate the irate lackey. Not to mention—" He broke off as he realised that Penny hadn't heard a word he'd been saying. "What is it?"

"I—I'm not sure." Her shoulders had hunched. "I thought I heard—no, never mind."

"Are you cold?" He spoke so sharply that it jerked her attention back to him.

"Cold? In this weather? Don't be an idiot. No, I thought I heard someone singing." Her eyes went suddenly dreamy. "There it is again, someone humming, a man. Listen! Oh, lovely! Don't you hear it?"

Ringan, staring at her, felt a reminiscent thrill of cold down his back. This time, it was merely a normal reaction to something he didn't understand; except for birdsong and muted traffic noise, the room was absolutely quiet. He heard nothing at all.

"No," he said. "I don't hear anything." Something strange in Penny's stance caught his eye and held it. She looked puzzled, enraptured, as if her ears had been touched by music not meant for them to hear.

"Oh," she said, and her voice was stricken, "it's gone now. It was probably just someone's radio. Why are you looking at me like that?"

"Because the nearest radio—the nearest house, anyway—is Wych-sale House, a good mile away. You must have excellent ears, dear, which is hardly fair, considering that you're as tone-deaf as a sack of bricks. I heard nothing. But . . ."

"Would this by any chance have something to do with why you were so frightened down in the kitchen?"

"I was not frightened," he snapped, and caught himself. "Right, okay, I know, I'm being childish. I'm not fooling you and I'm definitely not fooling myself. Have it your own way. I was frightened."

"But why?" She'd got hold of his hand and was swinging it. "And what does it have to do with me thinking I heard someone humming?"

Ringan, feeling a complete fool, told her about the flash of cold he'd felt on the stairs, the sensations of weakness he'd suffered, the suspicion of a touch, of a breath at his back. To his relief, and certainly to his surprise, she took it perfectly seriously.

"You say it hit you." The deep-sunk eyes had narrowed to considering slits. "That makes it sound as if you felt it was directed at you. Personally, I mean. Deliberately."

"Well . . . yes. I know it sounds mad. But honestly, Pen, that's how it felt. And whatever it was, it took all the stiffener out of me . . ."

"Physically and emotionally." She was nodding. "Of course. Limp and clammy physically, drained and ready to keel over emotionally. Yes?"

"Bang on the money." He caught hold of her free hand and faced her. "If you don't very much mind my asking, what in the name of Old Scratch do you know about it?"

She looked genuinely surprised. "Isn't it obvious?"

"Not to me. Come along, Penny. Out with it. What exactly do you think it was?"

"You've got a ghost, that's all." She smiled gently at his dropped jaw, and turned to survey the room. "You're right, this is a beautiful room. You even get your own fireplace! No need to worry about heating bills, once winter comes along."

"Penelope Wintercraft-Hawkes, do you honestly mean to stand there and tell me that—"

"—tell you that I grew reading ghost stories and that this sounds as if it's right out of anyone from Mrs. Radcliffe on up? As a matter of fact, yes. Come along," she said cheerfully. "Let's go check your phone messages and put Lord Randall out on his stand. We don't want your lovely guitar getting all temperamental, and you know he gets moody if he's left sitting in his case too long. Also, I'd strongly suggest having a look round that tithe barn. After we've gone into Glastonbury or Street for some groceries, maybe we can pay a visit to your noble patron and see what he can tell us about just who, or what, might be haunting Lumbe's Cottage."

The barn remained unexplored that day. When Ringan recovered from Penny's bombshell, he stopped sputtering long enough to realise that he hadn't eaten since leaving London that morning. Penny, aware that a hungry Ringan tended to be short-tempered and uncooperative, promptly bundled him into her Jaguar and headed off toward Glastonbury in search of food.

By the time she had maneuvered the elegant car through the twisting country lanes and dodged huge lorries on the blind curves, they had reached the town itself and Penny, as hungry as Ringan, was beginning to snap and snarl. She nosed the Jag into a space outside a small café and pulled Ringan toward the source of the food they both craved.

After they had finished a leisurely meal, they were both in better moods and the long summer evening had begun its slow slide toward night. Emerging into a lovely shadowy dusk, Ringan linked his arm in Penny's, and suddenly laughed. Penny, replete and lazy, looked inquiring.

"I was thinking what a mad sort of day it's been," he told her. "I woke up in London in an overpriced rented bed-sit. I'm going to bed in Somerset in my own home. Which happens to be haunted."

"You're assuming I'm right." She sounded distracted; her eyes had found the outline of Glastonbury Abbey against the evening sky, a sight staggering enough to demand her full attention. "That's flattering, but don't take it as gospel. I could quite easily be wrong. Oh, Ringan, look at the Abbey! Now, if you told me that little lot was haunted, I'd have no trouble believing it. Where are we? Magdalene Street?"

"Magdalene Street it is." Together, they stared at the towering spikes of the ruined building where, legend says, Joseph of Arimathea planted his walking stick after the crucifixion and watched it flower into a thorn tree. The Abbey was indeed haunted ground, and had probably been so for centuries before Christ. Ringan, feeling Penny rub her cheek against his, aimed a quick kiss at her ear; something about that imposing pile demanded the reassurance of physical contact. "Shouldn't we go hunt up some shops?"

They did so, even remembering to get a bottle of wine for Albert Wychsale. Penny, mindful of the Jaguar's paint in the deepening shadows and unfamiliar with the roads, drove far more slowly than she had during the trip in. The road paced the boundaries of the Wychsale holdings, following the course of the Carlyon as it flowed toward the Brue.

Penny pulled off the road and parked on the lawn, next to Ringan's Alfa. It was now fully dark, and the sky was showing a canopy of early stars. With a sigh of relief and a silent vow to inspect her precious paintwork in the morning, she got out and began unloading the groceries. Beside her, Ringan was a mere indigo outline.

"There should be five bags," Penny murmured. She kept her voice hushed; in the still country air, volume would have been jarring. A bird, an owl or perhaps a nightjar, called out from the trees across the river; a late cricket rattled spasmodically, and was abruptly silent again. "I've got three of them, and I think you've got the one with the eggs. Mind you don't—oh!"

The last word was a gasp. Ringan, halfway up the path to Lumbe's Cottage, wheeled round.

"What's wrong?"

"Something—something brushed my legs," she replied shakily. She stood immobile, willing her eyes to adjust to the darkness. After a moment they did, and Ringan caught her light laugh and saw her kneel.

"Penny?"

"Hullo, you handsome old thing, you," she said. It took Ringan a startled moment to realise that she wasn't talking to him. "You frightened me half out of my wits. Where on earth did you come from?"

Ringan set the groceries down and made his way back to her side. When he saw her companion, a magnificent Persian cat, he grinned to himself and knelt beside her.

"Top of the evening, Butterball. Out on the prowl, are you, mate?"

The enormous beast purred with a deep contented rumble, making beguiling little cat motions, batting at Penny's caressing fingers with his paws and ducking his head under his own leg. Ringan caught the flash of Penny's teeth in the moonlight as she smiled.

"Butterball?" she asked with some amusement. The cat, apparently recognising his own name, trilled at her. "What a perfect name for this creature, he must weigh twenty pounds. What is he, the official Wychsale House feline ornament?"

"Don't try convincing him of that. He thinks he owns the house, the land, and probably the bloody county."

"Of course he does, he's a cat. Pretty baby, pretty monster kitty beast," Penny crooned. "Good Lord, he's an absolute cushion. I take it you've met him before?"

"He used to keep me company while I was working on the manor house, you know, the way cats help."

"Meaning, of course, that he drove you mental. Shedding on your papers, making bread on your knees, or simply chasing the laces on your shoes?"

"All of the above, and then some. You know, that's one of the things I like about Wychsale. He's a cat person. I always think of the English as surrounding themselves with spaniels or corgis or those hideous things the Queen raises." Ringan scratched the cat behind one ear, reducing him to a limp puddle of fur and generating a frenzy of purrs. "You think he's handsome in the dark, just wait till you see him in a good light. He's a cameo shade Persian. Golden fur, golden eyes, everything about him bright and shining. A matinee idol, and he knows it. Come on, let's get this stuff sorted out and put away. Good thing we left the lights on. I wouldn't fancy stumbling about in the dark until I know the place better."

Butterball accompanied them, weaving between their legs and generally getting in the way. In the moonlight, the cottage had a bright, welcoming look to it. Ringan, busily loading the shelves of his fridge with butter and eggs and milk, suddenly thought that if a ghost was standing at his shoulder, the cat would surely know it . . .

"You know," Penny remarked as she pulled a carton marked "crockery" from the pile against the wall and efficiently unpacked it, "if the old tales about animals being aware of ghosts are true, either the house is clear at this moment, or this beast is a twit."

Ringan jumped about a foot. "I was just thinking that very thing. Do you suppose the old stories are true? And are you making tea, or just fussing with the kettle?"

"I'm making tea, and if you want a nice cuppa, just say the word." At Ringan's nod, she rinsed an extra cup. "That question you asked, that was silly. And you a folklorist! Shame on you."

"Meaning?"

"Meaning that all old wives' tales have some basis in fact. A truism gets to be a truism because at least some bits of it have been observed to be true, and you know, love, back in the bad old days, a wife didn't live long enough to get old if she wasn't paying serious attention. I'd bet a few bob on animals knowing when something's off somewhere."

"Then I've just had a nice bright idea." He picked up Butterball, grunting with the effort. "Woof, this beast is a case of back strain looking for a place to happen. How long until that kettle boils?"

"Five minutes, maybe ten. I filled it all the way up." She'd already figured out what he had in mind. "Were you planning on using him as a distant early warning system? A canary in a coal mine, so to speak?"

"Clever lass. That I am. Come along, fat cat, let's go sniff at Uncle Ringan's bonny, bonny bed and see if there's anything nasty lurking about."

" 'Make my bed, mammy, do,' " Penny quoted from the song "Lord Randall," and followed man and feline up the stairs. "Which reminds me, did you happen to bring any sheets down from London with you? Any linen on that bed upstairs has most likely been there since the *Titanic* went down. How's Butterball holding up?"

"All quiet on the western front, at least so far." The huge golden cat, nestled in Ringan's arms, showed no emotion stronger than general smugness at being carried. As Penny opened each door, Ringan brought Butterball in and waited for some display of uneasiness. The cat stretched his neck, looking obligingly at each room in succession before immediately losing interest. There was no unnatural cold, and no distant humming. If Albert Wychsale's cat was to be believed, all was as it should be.

In the master bedroom, Ringan set Butterball on the floor. The cat immediately jumped onto the bed, kneading fastidiously in the center of the antique quilt and collapsing into a contented ball of golden hair.

"Well," Penny said, "I feel safer already. I wonder if this bed is half as comfortable as Butterball would have us believe. Or would he purr like that even if he was lying in a nettle patch?" She sat down beside the cat, and stretched out on her back. "My God, Ringan, it's a feather mattress! Probably musty, dusty, and mouldy under this nice bit of quilting. Hadn't we better take a look?"

"It doesn't smell musty." Ringan's eyebrows had drawn together, and his beard was jutting. Penny knew that look; it meant he was concentrating. "In fact, I'd say—what is that smell? It's awfully familiar, somehow."

"All I smell is Butterball, your basic eau de damp kitty. I suspect he went hunting near the river before deigning to visit us." Something in Ringan's stance, beard bristling and warlike, shoulders stiff, made her prop herself up on one elbow. "What's the matter? Here, what are you doing?"

"Get up a moment, will you? There. Stand still. Now breathe in, and tell me what you smell."

She stood beside him, eyes open, willing to humour him. The room was deliciously warm, everything was as it should be; the painted ceiling and prettily papered walls, the wooden floor with a tendency to creak if weight was injudiciously applied near the two dormer windows, the windows themselves, with their leaded glass and weathered shutters. The fireplace, obligingly cleaned at some point in the past and not used since. The exquisite furniture, coated with dust. The bright yellow cat, who lay in the center of the bed and watched her with feline curiosity, his round eyes as liquid as molten gold. And a smell, a lovely poignant smell, drifting in from the garden to bathe her and soothe her and calm her until she felt at peace, at rest . . .

"Penny?"

She didn't hear him. Her eyes, which had narrowed to drugged-looking slits, were fixed on the cat.

Butterball made a long, interested sound in his throat. Persians do not bristle when startled or frightened, as do their smooth-coated cousins. Yet, through some alchemy of his species, he had become larger as he watched her. The innocuous, soothing purr becoming something else, a trill, a growl, an invitation to something unknown, and beneath him, something shimmered with a colour that came from somewhere else, lively lines, a face, hair as black as Penny's own, a picture of . . .

"Penny!"

She came out of it, her mouth dry and her eyes watering. Unnoticed, the cat relaxed. Ringan had been right; the smell was still there, strong and potent. Even as she put a name to it, it began to fade.

"Lavender," she said, her voice shaky. "It's lavender. But there's no lavender growing outside, is there?"

"None that I'm aware of. Penny, are you all right? You've gone the colour of . . ."

"I have to sit down," she remarked, and promptly did. The floor creaked beneath her as she let herself settle. In a vague, surprised way, she found that her knees had ceased functioning. The palms of her hands, where they lay flat against the parquet, were slick with a clammy sweat. Her breath was coming in small shallow catches.

Ringan sat down beside her, his eyes on her face.

"Hullo," she told him. "Fancy meeting you here. So kind of you to come down."

"Always a pleasure, ducks." He touched her cheekbone with the tip of a finger. "Ah. You're looking a bit more human. What in hell was all that about?"

"How should I know? Oh, you mean how I felt? Limp, drained, relaxed beyond belief. Not scared, though. Most definitely not scared. I didn't feel any sense of threat, or jeopardy, or any of that rubbish."

"Then how did you feel?"

"A bit sad—no, wrong word." Penny brushed a stray hair off her brow and inspected the tips of her fingers. "Oh, good, I've stopped sweating. You know how I hate unexpected sweating; it's so tacky. Not sad, really; more like wistful. Forlorn. Bittersweet, like cooking chocolate that's had the bloom go off it. You know?"

Oddly enough, he did; the bizarre description made perfect sense. He put an arm around her shoulders. "There's altogether too much going on around this place. For my first day as squire, it's hardly fair. Tell me, did you see the cat? Because I wasn't watching him."

"If you mean, did he react, yes he did. He seemed to be, well, concentrating on me. Pacing me, almost. And his pupils kept getting smaller and smaller . . ."

"So did yours. Absolute pinpricks." Ringan got to his feet and offered Penny a hand. "All right, it's official; we've got a ghost. So let me ask you an important question, my lamb. Do you think we're safe to sleep in this chamber of diffused horrors? Because if you don't, we'll drive into Glastonbury and rent a room at a bed and breakfast and tomorrow we'll hire an exorcist and send the bills for both to the Right Honourable."

" 'Chamber of diffused horrors,' " she said appreciatively. "A lovely phrase. I don't think a room at the inn will be required, Ringan. Whatever else I felt, I felt safe. Our ghost is not dangerous or bad-tempered."

From below came the whistle of the kettle. Butterball, who knew that where there was tea for humans there was likely cream for cats, jumped off the bed, gave one wildly elongating stretch, and headed down the stairs. As they followed, Ringan leading the way, Penny spoke up behind him.

"I wonder why this place is called Lumbe's Cottage," she said thoughtfully. "Was the original occupant called Lumbe, do you suppose?"

"Since the original occupants were little better than serfs, I doubt they'd have had the cheek to hang a shingle with their name over the door. I'd imagine it has something to do with the local pronunciation of 'loom,' but don't quote me." Ringan, pleased to have negotiated the dark staircase without accident, pushed open the kitchen door. "Remind me to get a doorstop for this thing. Whoever they were, those tenants, they probably worked for the Right Honourable Whoever Wychsale of the day; Piers, I think his name was. He owned the textile mill downriver. I remember that from the records. Why?"

"Oh, nothing. Curiosity; I wanted to know, that's all." Penny accepted a cup of tea and gratified Butterball by pouring him a saucer of milk. "Just like fat cat here."

"Just remember what curiosity did to the original cat in the story."

"Somehow," Penny said cheerfully, "I doubt that's going to be a problem."

Three

*My father to me scornful said
How could you fancy a factory maid,
When you could have girls fine and gay,
Dressed like unto the Queen of May?*

Penny woke the next morning to a rosy sunrise, and the sound of birdsong in the Wychsale apple trees.

Ringan's first day of tenancy had ended without further incident. It had been a strange day, she thought drowsily, particularly for Ringan. After all, how often does one move into a new home and discover that it's haunted? She herself had been conscious of the feeling she associated with jet lag, or of coming home after a long stay in a strange place; familiar things look different, and a sense of place is skewed or absent.

Penny, limp and relaxed under the quilt, felt her face curve into a satisfied smile. Neither the imminence of a possible ghost nor spatial disorientation had stopped them making love as they hadn't done in years. If Lumbe's Cottage did harbor something supernatural, it also packed a potent aphrodisiacal wallop. She couldn't remember the last time Ringan had been so physically aware, or so aggressive. Every muscle in her body was talking, and that was saying something, considering the physical effort demanded by her profession. Lugging props and demonstrating sword fights for the understudies did not make for a delicate physique. Ringan had given her a proper old workout. If, by any chance, the ghost was going to spice up their sex life, it could damned well stay here, and welcome. In fact, she'd fight any attempt at exorcising it tooth and nail. Last night had been absolutely sensational.

She glanced affectionately at Ringan. He was miles deep and, from the look of it, sleeping peacefully. She herself had expected disturbances, whether from nightmares or gusts of spectral lavender wafting in through the window she wasn't sure. Nothing had happened; if anything had gone bump in the night, she'd slept through it. Actually, she'd slept like a rock. Penny, like most intelligent people, dreamed vividly and often. Whatever had wandered through her subconscious during the hours of darkness hadn't disturbed her at all. She felt rested, happy, and ready to take on the world.

She was also hungry, which surprised her; Penny could rarely face more than a cup of tea before noon. She slipped quietly out of bed, taking care not to wake Ringan. Then, after throwing on her robe and using the loo, she padded softly downstairs to make some tea.

The idea to surprise Ringan with an herb omelet in bed came naturally, and left her feeling vastly pleased with herself. It certainly would surprise him, she thought; she was definitely not the domestic type. Still, they'd bought eggs and milk and butter in town the night before. The herbs would be fresh from the garden; they would taste of the morning sun, and leave the memory of her like a deep kiss at the back of his palate. Yes, she'd make him an omelet. It would make a nice beginning to a whole new day, and allow her to indulge in a kind of practical witchcraft as well.

But not before a nice cup of tea for herself. She plugged in the kettle and waited, pouncing on the OFF switch before its whistling could wake Ringan. Then, cup in hand, she opened the doors and stepped out into the morning.

While Penny and Ringan had both grown up in the country, she had never come to consider herself a city-dweller. Her childhood, spent in a rambling old house near Gloucester, had been idyllic. Like Ringan, Penny had spent her youth playing in the countryside with her brother and sister; unlike Ringan, she'd spent those years surrounded by money as well as siblings. The family's home at Whistler's Croft, a late Elizabethan manor house in Hampshire, was beautifully kept, and updated with modern comforts the moment they became available.

The memories evoked by this Somerset garden, therefore, were happy enough. Of the three Wintercraft-Hawkes children, only her brother Stephen had abandoned fields and streams for concrete and tower blocks. And he'd had no choice, really; his job had taken him to Hong Kong. He still came home to stay whenever he could.

Sipping tea, letting her memory wander, Penny stood barefoot in the garden. She was happy, in the clear, rarified way that is a special gift of first light. The grass was moist with dew, which would burn off before noon. The fresh, still air smelled of herbs and earth and wildflowers. And the sun, touching the thatched roof of the still unexplored barn, provided a charming view, worthy of any post-card.

That barn, now; she must ask Ringan about it. Something was not quite right there. There was a Tudor long barn not a mile from her parents' home, and it was four times the size of this one. In fact, she'd never seen a tithe barn so small, and she'd seen several. Was it possible that Ringan, the expert on period architecture, had gotten his facts jumbled?

Still, that could wait. She finished her tea, went back indoors long enough to set the cup down, and reemerged into the garden with a saucer and a knife. In a state of contentment, she squatted down among the plants and began to select herbs. Her thoughts wandered happily from point to trivial point: her sister Candida's venture into beekeeping; the stark, effective stage design she had planned for the Tamburlaine Players Copenhagen stint in July; just how much hot water it would take to fill the tub upstairs and whether it would stay hot once it was filled. She never once thought about the unnerving possibility of ghosts on the premises.

It was only after she had twice caught herself humming aloud that she realised her voice was one-half of a duet.

Penny, as Ringan had reminded her, was tone-deaf. She minded the fact dreadfully, and she would have given up several important things—her looks, her iron digestion, even her eye for detail—

without a second thought, had the gods only seen fit to give her the ability to make music. She loved music, in the primal, emotional fashion that has gone out of style in this age of synthesizers and digital sampling. Music touched her feelings; it reduced her to her most basic, and purest, self. It echoed in the pit of her stomach, that place where the Chinese say the soul is found.

The problem was, she couldn't produce it; she couldn't even reproduce what she'd heard. This made her the Wintercraft-Hawkes family anomaly. Her father was a pianist, and her mother not only played the harp, but sang like a lark. Neither Candy nor Stephen could read music, yet both could sit down at a piano and play from memory; harmony, it seemed, was the glorious genetic birthright of an already privileged family. Only Penny, who of them all loved music the best and most deeply, had been denied even the ability to hum a tune without her voice flatting out to an unpleasant drone. While her speaking voice was deep and lovely, her singing voice was a hideous, atonal mess. Something in the construction between brain and ear had gone awry in the womb. This lack was the root of her passion for classical theatre; dramatic verse is music with meter and harmony, but without scales. Shakespeare and Sophocles had written songs that allowed her to sing without music.

Someone was singing now. She stood barefoot among the wet spikes of mint and rosemary, her head cocked to one side, listening intently. This was the same voice that had pulled a response from her yesterday afternoon. Ringan had said it was not a radio, and he'd been right. It was a man's voice, a deep resonant baritone. It seemed to come from everywhere, and from nowhere. It was close, yet far away. And it was humming, a tune that Penny heard clearly, a melody without words; sad, redolent of loss and regret, heartrending and painful.

"Come along," she said quietly to the empty garden. She supposed that she ought to be frightened, but all she felt was a deep desire to track down the author of this melancholy music, and to comfort him. "Come along, then. It's quite all right, I won't hurt you. Where are you?"

The humming faltered, broke off, and began again. Penny closed her eyes, knowing instinctively that this was the way to find the source; she would see nothing with her workaday vision. She made herself relax. She waited.

Obligingly, a picture came. She saw a room with an earthen floor, dim, offering little natural light. A cool room. A majestic curving pair of beams, oak by the look of them, weathered by many years to a gnarled gray that looked like stone. Supports along the walls, evenly spaced, load-bearing. They were supporting the ceiling. A roof. In one corner of this cool, shadowy place was a pile of sacks. Hay sacks? Flour sacks? She couldn't quite see. Or were they sacks, after all? There seemed to be a touch of vivid colour in there, too bright, too defined, to be the dull burlap of grain bags. Or perhaps it was just a trick of what light there was.

But she could smell the place, quite clearly. Dust in the air, the faded sour tang of earth packed down by use and the pressure of feet, and thatch . . .

The picture faded. Penny opened her eyes and found herself staring at the eastern boundary of Ringan's property. Sitting squarely in her view was the weirdly diminutive tithe barn, with its roof of thatch.

From Albert Wychsale's apple orchard, a bird called out sharply. Penny set the herbs she'd gathered on the ground. Gathering the skirts of her robe in one hand, oblivious to stones and insects and whatever else might threaten her bare feet, she went swiftly across the garden.

The barn was slightly larger than Lumbe's Cottage, and in places obviously predated it by many years. Penny was no expert, but there was no mistaking the age of the foundation stones, darker by far than the Somerset golden stone used for the rest of the walls. The older layer came up to Penny's shoulders; dry and cold, they looked as though they had never felt the sun.

She stood in deep shadow beneath the overhanging eaves and touched the topmost edge of the foundation. Whatever had been used as weatherproofing between those cut stones was not nearly so modern as caulk or plaster. Dung, she thought, sheep or cow dung.

What did they call it down here? Wattle and daub, was it? Cob? That must be it. It was the consistency of ancient rock, as hard as dinosaur bones, with tiny pebbles and bits of straw forever trapped within its mass.

Keeping quite still, she waited for the voice again. As if reading a cue card, it obliged. Odd, she thought with detachment, very odd indeed. The voice was no louder than it had been, and sounded no closer. Yet she had no doubt that the barn was its source. The awareness of that fact tingled in her stomach, deep and clear as the humming voice itself.

Penny circled the barn, memorizing its features. There were two windows, small and securely shuttered. Remembering what she knew of such buildings, she looked for slits cut into the walls, and then realised that with the comparative newness of the upper stones, such slits would be unlikely. Yet, perhaps because of that ancient foundation, she got no sense of modernity. Something about the place spoke of age, perhaps a greater age than Ringan had thought. The very ground beneath her bare feet breathed antiquity.

She turned a corner and found herself at the barn door. The sound of water, a soft steady trickle, touched her ears. For a moment she thought that someone had left a sink running inside the barn itself. Then she realised that the voice of the water came from some ten feet beyond the eastern wall of the building. It was a stream, constant and quiet and yet somehow viscerally present, perhaps the source of running water for Lumbe's Cottage itself.

She laid her hand on the latch, gripped it, and twisted it hard to one side.

With that contact, pictures flooded her mind. They came too fast and shadowy to define, or make sense of.

A group of men, seemingly wrapped in rags and leather, men that were blurred, vital only in their movements. A long table. The smell of fire, and of cooking, and of sweat. More movement, sensed and somehow heard rather than seen, and then true sound; human voices shouting, calling out, laughing, making words Penny could hear but not understand. There were animal voices as well, a noisy swell of bleats and neighs and squawks, and straw on the floor. Counterpointing it all was the light, steady pulse of running water.

These impressions were brief, and were replaced by fresh visions and sounds. Different men, still indistinct in feature and frame, but clearer than those who had come before. They were dressed in a way Penny could recognise; long curling hair, fantastic hats, clothing that had been exquisitely finicky when new, now torn and stained with the rigors of the chase. They were alert, shoulders hunched and ears cocked for sound. These were hiding men, hunted men, men who knew that to relax their vigilance for a moment could mean capture and death. And still the voice of moving water declared itself over it all.

A swirl, a fade. A third picture, brilliantly clear.

A man, sitting on the barn floor. He held something in his hands, something his fingers worked without pause, touching, stroking. A musical instrument? Strain though she would, Penny couldn't quite identify it; she could see only that it was small and squarish in shape. Next to him was something that looked like a makeshift bed, no more than a length of sack or rush matting, tucked carefully around something lumpy. Something about the texture made Penny think it was probably filled with straw. Someone had rested on that bed, and not long ago, either. It still retained the distinct outlines of a human form.

More than an outline—was that someone sleeping there, a face, a swirl of black hair, a hand reaching out? For a moment Penny felt her heart clutch and freeze, for it looked to be herself in that bed, oddly flattened, a rag doll of a woman with all the stuffing gone out of her. Then Penny realised that she was looking at a picture of life, and not life itself; the woman in the bed was scarcely more than doll-sized.

The man's hands grew quiet. Setting whatever he held on the floor beside him, he reached out and laid one palm on the bed. The gesture was gentle, light, loving. It spoke eloquently of tenderness.

Make my bed, mammy, do, Penny thought clearly. Lord Randall's plea after he's been poisoned, but that's not what he was humming; I'd have recognised that tune. The poor sod, the poor sorry old sod. He's had a lover on that mouldy old bed, and now she's gone off somewhere, and he's missing her quite dreadfully. The poor old . . .

The man lifted his head and looked straight at her.

Fascinated, she stared back at him, her theatre-trained eye automatically mapping his features. She'd called him old, but that was wrong; he wasn't old at all. Despite lines of care around his eyes, he couldn't have been much over twenty. He had a strong neck, broad cheekbones, and curling brown hair. His mouth was generous, bracketed with those same lines that came with worry or hard work. His nose was bumpy, broken at some point and poorly healed. Everything about him spoke of the artisan classes, neither upper class nor peasant. Here was ten generations of solid British yeomanry, come together in one country-bred package.

Still staring directly into Penny's face, he opened his mouth and spoke. A word came out, a name.

Betsy.

The name hung in the air like an echo of sad perfume, quavered, and then dissipated. A moment later, so did the entire scene.

When Ringan hurried out of Lumbe's Cottage and found her a few minutes later, Penny was still standing at the barn door. She was alternately pounding on the door and pulling futilely at the locked latch. Tears were streaming down her cheeks, and she was whimpering.

"Look, run this past me again, will you, love? You said he actually called out a name?"

"Betsy. Her name is—was—Betsy." Penny swallowed a mouthful of tea and decided that come hell or high water, they were buying chairs for the kitchen today. She'd been leaning up against the Welsh dresser and answering Ringan's questions for a half hour, gulping down cups of the hot sweet liquid he kept pouring for her. Her legs were tired, and her hip was sore from its sustained contact with the dresser's sharp edge.

Between sips and answers, she'd been trying to sort out her feelings, which were mixed and maddeningly contradictory. She was hollow with the need for food, but the thought of eating was nauseating. She wanted to cry, but she was exhilarated, too. Mostly, though, she was thirsty and tired of standing. She was also warm. How could Ringan possibly have felt cold in the presence of that long-gone singer? She thought she might never feel cold again.

"And you could see him clearly. Right." Ringan set his own cup down on the dresser. "I must buy some chairs for this room," he said irrelevantly. "Remind me, will you? Okay, let's move on. A yeoman, you said. A young bloke, probably peasant stock. But not a labourer? Not a field-worker or a cowman or whatnot?"

She shook her head. "Too well dressed for that. Definitely a cut above. And his hands were lovely, well-kept. Wrong sort of calluses."

"And he was dressed early nineteenth century? You're sure about that?"

"I'm a theatrical producer, darling. We do period plays. I handle all the research and design all the costumes. Remember? I do know a little bit about period clothing. Trust me, these were homespuns from the early nineteenth." The stream, she thought, the flowing water. It was puzzling. Why had it been the only constant that she could hear? It had run through the entire succession of images like a common thread in some bizarre historical quilt. Was it just coincidence, or was it important? And if it was important, why?

"Sorry, Pen. I'm just trying to make sure we've got it all straight. No need to get shirty. Here, why in hell are we standing about? Give your legs a rest." Ringan sat down on the floor. She sat gratefully beside him, trying to ease her tired back. He put an arm around her shoulders, and said thoughtfully, "Do you know what I find really interesting about all this?"

"That you felt cold and I felt warm?"

"Not precisely." Penny had relaxed. Her relaxation came through her skin to him, moving through his own flesh, taking him under its mantle as well. He let himself succumb to it, pushing aside the tension and worry that had covered him since that first moment on the stairs. *Not scared,* he thought, but the thought was idle, lazy.

The situation was mad, Ringan thought, completely mad. It was a sunny June morning in Somerset, birds were singing, plants were growing, people were undoubtedly going about their daily business. Yet here they were, sitting on the floor and discussing a ghost in a barn. Could an introduction to the joys of home ownership get any stranger? "It was that we had such different reactions to the same stimulus. I could feel it, and I felt cold and, well, spooked. The word 'unpleasant' doesn't do it justice. You could hear it, and all you felt was warm, and a desire to help the poor sod. In fact, you seemed completely entranced by the whole thing."

"Believe me, I'd already noticed the difference." Penny carefully shifted her legs, which were tingling. "Although I don't know why you say 'entranced.' But what's your point?"

"Well," he said carefully, "in light of our extremely different reactions, and taking into account the disparate nature of the phenomena involved, not to mention the fact that they seem to occur in different places . . ."

"Oh, stow all that pedantic rubbish and give it to me straight," she said, exasperated. "Two ghosts. You think we've got two ghosts. That's it, isn't it?"

"Two ghosts," he said, and beamed at her. "And that, for some reason, we can each only sense one of them. You clever old thing, you. Give the little lady a coconut. Or would you rather have a nice bottle of Ghost-Be-Gone?"

Penny snickered, but immediately sobered. "All right, I'll buy it. After all, two ghosts is no more ludicrous or unlikely than one ghost. If I'm going to accept the idea of a ghost at all—and after this morning, I defy anyone not to accept it—then I'll take your idea as a working start. In for a penny, in for tuppence. Although I'm not so certain about that whole 'only sensing one' bit, unless you think the boy in the barn is responsible for the lavender in the house. Still, where does that leave us? The idea of two ghosts, I mean? And I still want to know who you chose that word 'entranced.'"

Ringan stretched out on his back and cupped his hands beneath his head. "I think it's obvious that the ghost you've been hearing is the chap in the barn. I mean, you actually saw him, and heard his voice."

"I did indeed, and a whole film festival of other scenes as well. Don't forget that. He came the clearest, and he was the one I reacted to most strongly. But the others were there too; it was as though the barn was an *avant garde* movie house, or a bizarre collage or something. Those cavaliers, for example. Lovelocks, feathered hats, absolutely enormous cuffs on their coats, and those boots . . . they were cavaliers, all right. I couldn't make out what that first lot was wearing, but it seemed to be composed mainly of badly tanned dead animals. In fact, if the sound effects were anything to go by, they kept their potential wardrobes in the house with them." Out of nowhere, a wave of exhaustion hit Penny broadside. She lay down on the floor and snuggled up against Ringan. "So?"

"So, light o' my life, never mind about the ancient rustics and the nervous blokes with the bonny yellow curls. What I want to know is, who's the second ghost, the one that gave me the cauld grues on the stairs yesterday?"

"Betsy," Penny said positively. "It must be this Betsy bird he was singing about. I'll bet she was who I saw in that nasty bit of hay out there, as well. If you felt her in the house, then maybe she lived here. Oh!"

"The lights go on at last," Ringan said smugly. "Allow me to recap, as the executioner said to the guillotined hatmaker. If she was this singing chap's lady love, and if she lived in this cottage, and if you can put an approximate date on the clothes he was wearing . . ."

"I can," Penny said firmly. "Waterloo, or close to it. Call it somewhere around 1815, give or take half a decade in either direction."

". . . then we can take a dekko at those papers in the Wychsale House muniment room and find out who these people are, I mean were."

"Aha, a plan. We progress. Ouch, I must move." Penny rolled over and sat up, rubbing her hip. "I don't believe I'm lying on the floor—why am I doing that? Ringan . . ."

"I know," he said quietly. "I used the word entranced, but I might just as easily have said ensorceled. I meant entranced as in, gone into a trance. You looked as though you were trying to walk into the middle of a fairy story, or climb Rapunzel's hair, or go straight up a beanstalk. You didn't look normal. You didn't look right. You simply weren't completely here, and what got to me most was that you didn't seem to even want to be here." He heard his own voice slide up the scale and take on a dark, urgent resonance. "And I didn't like it. It's got to stop. You belong here, not—wherever you were."

They looked at each other. Penny laid a hand on his arm.

"It's all right," she told him. "I'm all right. I'm right here, Ringan. I don't feel that anything is trying to suck me in, or take me over, or any of that. And I'm not frightened, not yet, anyway; if and when I do start getting frightened, I'll tell you, I swear. All right?"

He sighed, a long exhale. "All right. For now, all right."

"Good. Then let's get down to real-world business, shall we?" She smiled at him. "Before we march up to the manor and bait the Right Honourable in his posh den, there are three things I want to do first."

Ringan stood up and helped Penny to her feet. "What?"

"First, I want a mouthful of breakfast. I do believe my appetite's about to come roaring back."

"I'm hungry too," Ringan said. He had regained his good cheer. "I'll even cook the eggs, since you were kind enough to root up that pile of herbs over there . . ."

"Also," she interrupted firmly, "I shall have a bath. My feet are dirty."

"I don't believe you've got dirty feet. You're just curious about that vast tub affair."

"And lastly, I want to find the key to the barn and see what's inside."

Ringan, mixing eggs and milk in a large bowl, turned and regarded her. Her voice had undergone a subtle but definite change. "You think the barn's going to be that important?" he asked quietly.

She nodded. Ringan set the bowl down and turned for the main room.

"Where are you going?"

"For my keys." Ringan pushed the kitchen door open, disappeared into the tiny hall, and came back with a bunch of keys in one hand. "You think the barn might offer up some answers. Believe me, love, I'm not about to argue, not after that freak show you went through."

"All right," Penny sighed. "But let's change the order of events. I still want to eat first, but I'll save the bath for last. The inside of that barn may not have had a good dusting in centuries. Where did we put the bread, and the butter? I want toast. Two slices, please."

"Here, I've got it." Ringan sounded distracted. "You know, lamb, there's a fourth item on the agenda. We ought to check in at Wychsale House and pump the Right Hon."

"Waste of time, if you ask me." Penny pushed bread into the toaster. "If he'd known the place was haunted, or if he was willing to admit it, he'd have said so when he was trying to jockey you into taking it on. Wouldn't he?"

"Well, he did say that Lumbe's Cottage had quite a history. But I wasn't thinking so much about that." Ringan rubbed a hand over his beard, a gesture that meant his mind was sorting out options. "I was wondering about the previous tenants, the ones who might still be alive."

"Alive?" She gaped at him. "Are you out of your mind? They'd be about a hundred and fifty years old."

"No, no. I meant the tenants during the Second World War, not the Napoleonic Wars."

"Oh." Penny began buttering toast. "That's right, you said something about this place being used by the army in the early forties. I'd forgotten that. It's a damned good notion, too—it would be a long shot, but it's possible. And we could get the information without tipping off your noble patron, if you'd rather keep this between us for now."

"How?" The words were indistinct; Ringan was wolfing down toast as he scrambled eggs with his free hand.

"We contact the army, of course. If the Right Hon can be tricked into disgorging a few names without demanding to know why, fine. But if he can't, or if he can't remember any particular names, we could always check the records and find out which branch of the military hung out here. What do you think? Here, give me some of that egg, you greedy lout."

"Lout yourself." Ringan took a bite of his own cookery and made a satisfied noise. "Quite nice, if I do say so myself. Your idea, Penny love, is not so dusty. In fact, it's damned good. I doubt that our Albert will have any useful memories; during the Battle of Britain he was little Bertie, if he wasn't Albert the Embryo. But a good long in-depth gaze at the records should give us all the names we need."

"Then we have a plan. Goody." The food must have been what she needed, Penny thought. She was reviving so much that the idea of actually entering the barn was perceptibly less unnerving. "So we finish eating, wash up, get dressed, and see what's inside Thatch Central."

"Followed by a hot bath for two, a courtesy call at the manor house, and a mad hunt for suitable chairs in Glastonbury proper. It's going to be a long day. Jesus!"

Something had scratched at the kitchen door. Penny laughed, set her empty plate in the sink, and swung the bottom half of the door wide.

"It's only Butterball, come to pay us a morning call. Fresh from his morning stroll and in search of his second or third meal of the day, no doubt." The cat saluted her by bumping against her foot. She scratched between his ears, and watched as he moved on to Ringan. "I wonder if he'd like to come and sniff out the ghosts in the barn with us."

"What, this upper-class nitwit? You must be joking. Offer him a bowl of milk and a bite of your egg and he'd follow you to downtown Beirut. Wouldn't you, you overfed pampered lump, you?" Butterball, responding to the caressing tone, ignored this insult. He waited while Penny poured him a saucer of milk, acknowledged her with a slow blink of his golden eyes, and lapped contentedly. Penny watched him for a moment, and then turned toward the main room.

"I'm going upstairs to get dressed," she announced. "I've already been to the barn in my nightie, and I'm damned if I'll do that again."

It was nearly ten when Penny and Ringan, both dressed in yesterday's clothes, made their way across the green lawn. Butterball, held firmly in Penny's arms for the first few feet, now paced behind them; he'd indicated, by the use of gentlemanly but emphatic wriggles, that while he was willing to accompany them if they so desired, he'd rather walk. Since the garden was humming with caterpillars and dragonflies, there was something for him to pounce on every few feet. As Ringan said, that translated to kitty heaven.

They came to the barn doors and stood for a moment. Each was silent, busy with their own thoughts. Penny was remembering the flashes of vision, and wondering about the intense feeling of sympathy they had roused in her. Ringan, more prosaically, was regretting that he hadn't delved a bit more deeply into the existing paperwork on this peculiar building. It was quite possible that his new property was worth even more than Wychsale had thought. If he knew anything at all about architecture, the foundations of this pile had been standing before William and his Norman knights had shown up for the party at Hastings in 1066 . . .

"Come on," Penny said softly. "Let's get on with it."

Ringan studied the door. The latch was modern, probably installed during the army's tenure at Lumbe's. A good strong latch made sense; they'd likely used the barn for storage, perhaps communications equipment. The manor house had been used as a hospital for the Allied Forces recovering wounded, as well as to house evacuees from London during the Blitz.

The door wasn't modern. But was it the original entry? When had this heavily hinged plank been added? Hard to tell.

"Ringan?" Penny sounded nervous, almost edgy. "Please can we get on with it?"

He started. "Sorry. I was just wondering if my noble patron knew what he was giving up when he upped the ante with a Saxon barn."

"Saxon?" Penny was thoroughly startled. "Are you sure, Ringan? These upper walls are more recent than that, I would have thought. And wouldn't it be listed as a historic building, or protected building, or whatever the National Trust calls it?"

"The upper walls, yes. But either the base is Saxon, or I'm losing my touch. It doesn't matter, not at the moment. I mean, it's not really relevant to our immediate problem." He found the key he wanted and took a deep breath. "Here we go, then."

The key slipped easily into the bolt, and turned as if it had been recently oiled. There were no gothic-sounding screeches of rusty metal, no cobwebs, no touches from Poe or Stoker. Ringan pulled at the heavy door, and discovered that its massive iron hinges were equally cooperative. He swung it wide and stepped inside, Penny at his heels.

For a heart-stopping moment, he thought he'd walked into the shadowy world of Penny's morning visions. The dim cavern was full of shapes, some muffled, some sharp, all unexpected. He swallowed hard on a strangled gasp. Then his eyes adjusted to the gloom, and the gasp became a long, appreciative whistle.

Behind him, Penny had caught Butterball up in her arms. She had identified the contents of the barn a split second before Ringan did.

"Well, well." She spoke quietly, but Ringan could hear the relief in her voice. "It looks as though we won't have to shop for furniture after all."

The next ten minutes were spent in a pleasurable fairyland. They propped the huge door open and wrestled with the shutters, providing the room with a modicum of light. The barn's interior dimensions were precisely what Penny had seen and described earlier, right down to the four pairs of huge curving roof beams ("It's called a crucked roof, Pen, and what a beautiful example!"). Then they lifted sheets and dust covers from some of the loveliest furniture either of them had ever seen. Butterball got under their feet and generally made a nuisance of himself, finally settling on a discarded sheet to watch their activities with feline inscrutability.

"My word," Ringan said, when the last piece of furniture had been uncovered. "My word, my word."

"Which word would that be? No, never mind. I can probably guess." Penny stared at the treasure trove, but without Ringan's awe. "How long do you suppose this lot's been stashed away? A few weeks, a few years, what?"

"I don't know, lamb, but it would have to be a good long while." Ringan looked at his hands, smeared with grimy dust from the protective sheets. "The covers had a good inch of dust on them. Why?"

"Because none of the fabrics have rotted, that's why. Which means, if my needle-sharp wits are working properly, that this barn might be suitable for a music room after all."

"Explain yourself, wench."

"No damp, dearest fool. No smell of mildew, or mould. Which is very odd, considering . . ." Her voice trailed off. Ringan tore his gloating eyes from the past and future contents of his new home's main room and looked at her. There was a furrow between her fine brows.

"What is it?" Ringan asked sharply. "What's up? What's odd, and why?"

"Because of the stream." The furrow deepened. "How could so much water be running so close and not make the place damp? I mean, it never stops, does it?" She saw the confused look on his face, and blinked at him. "For heaven's sake, Ringan, can't you hear it?"

Ringan closed his eyes, straining into the quiet room. All he heard was their own breathing.

"No," he said finally. "I can't hear running water. If I remember correctly, the stream is about twenty feet away, up toward Wychsale House. Do you know, I wonder what it is that you're actually hearing, Penny."

"It's the stream." She had wrapped her arms tightly around herself. The gesture was primitive and atavistic, and it brought the memory of the cold he'd felt the day before back to Ringan with great clarity. "Loud, steady. I'm hearing moving water and I'm hearing it quite clearly, thank you. The way I heard it this morning, when I saw . . . oh, never mind. At least I'm not seeing anything unusual. Let us give thanks for small favours."

He stared at her for a moment, trying to understand the rasp in her voice, her constricted physical attitude, her bravado.

"Ringan," she said, and her voice trembled, "I'm frightened."

"It's all right, lamb. Don't be frightened, it's all right." Ringan was taken with a surge of tenderness, a sudden desire to protect. He gathered her into his arms and held her tightly. He was distantly aware that this behavior was unusual; both took their caresses seriously, and neither had a taste for stray hugs.

And Penny's response was as out of character as his own behaviour. She pressed herself up against him like a child, letting him feel her tremble as he stroked and soothed. Even as the protective urge swelled to a zenith, he thought, what in hell, what is all this? What are we doing? We're not acting like ourselves at all . . .

"Ringan?" Penny said in a very small voice. "Ringan, it's all right now. You can let go of me. It's over."

"What?" He heard how shaken he sounded, let go of Penny and stepped back, suddenly dizzy and disoriented. He managed to focus on her face, and saw that her eyes were stretched wide, and her face was strained and tense. "My God," he said weakly, "what *was* all that?"

"I don't know, at least I don't think I know. But there is one thing I do know."

"Good. That's absolutely smashing. I'm so glad one of us knows something." He went unsteadily toward the barn door, which had unaccountably swung shut. Surely they'd propped it open? "Actually, I know something too. I know I need air. Sweet clean air."

She followed him outside, standing quietly as he leaned against the weathered stuff of the walls, waiting for him to gulp his fill of warmth and light. Reality, she thought, the clear blessed light of day in the real world. One way or another, they were going to have to cope with this thing.

"So," Ringan said, recapturing her attention, "what, precisely, is it that you know?"

"It wasn't you. And it wasn't me."

He blinked at her. Somewhere nearby, a bee droned among the flowers that bordered the Wychsale gardens. Under it, behind it, the stream ran and danced. He could hear it plainly enough, now that he was outdoors.

"What do you mean?" he asked quietly. The question was unnecessary; he already knew what she meant. He felt the truth of it in his bones. Not me, he thought, not Penny.

"I saw him." Butterball came out and scent-marked her ankle. With seeming irrelevance, Penny wondered if that long-ago yeoman who had invaded her world had loved a cat of his own. She spoke sensibly and calmly. "When you were holding me. I opened my eyes and looked at your hands and they weren't your hands. They were the weaver's hands."

"The weaver? Betsy's lover? How do you know he was a weaver, Pen?"

"I looked down and they weren't your hands. And there was something on the floor, the same thing he was holding when I saw him in the barn this morning—that little square wooden thing. I'd thought it might be a musical instrument, but no. And now I know what it was." The bizarre jumble of words, spoken in Penny's reasonable and lilting voice, held a vast authority. "I thought it was a harp or something, a musical instrument. But I was wrong. It was a handloom."

Four

As for your fine girls, I don't care
If I could but enjoy my dear
I'd stand in the factory all the day
And she and I'd keep our shuttles in play.

"I've been thinking, Penny. You know, about what you saw? And it couldn't have been a handloom."

"Well, it was. Mind where you're going or you'll have that table on its side in the mud."

"Penny, I don't want to be a pill about this, but it couldn't have been. I may not raise silkworms for a living, but I do know that a handloom is not called a handloom because you can carry it about in your hand."

"You *are* being rather a pill, you know? I didn't mean a real, live, functional handloom. I'm not a halfwit, you know, and I do think you might give me some credit. Damn! It's slipping again. Lift your end a bit higher, would you? Ta."

Ringan, maintaining a sweaty grip on his end of a late Victorian hall table, complied. They'd emptied the barn of the bulk of its furniture cache, and the day had grown very warm. It was going to be a proper scorcher, Ringan thought, considering that it was still short of midday. He mentioned this to Penny, taking the opportunity to set the table down and wipe his brow. She was unsympathetic.

"Count your blessings, dearie, it might have been raining. Where are we putting this thing?"

"On the landing, under the stairway window." A vestige of

annoyance at being called a pill—his ego did not take kindly to Penny's disapproval—made him add caustically, "Maybe we can find a nice little handloom to put on it. For decoration, you know?"

Penny regarded him steadily for a moment. He was just familiar enough with that look to hastily add, "I'm sorry, darling. Very sorry indeed. That was rude and mean-spirited and you were wrong, I'm not a pill, I'm a plonker, a ninny, a twit. I'll belt up now."

"See that you do." There was cold steel in her tone. Ringan, hearing it, tensed and made ready to dive for cover. Penny's rare losses of temper tended to involve trips to the nearest casualty ward, and sometimes having to leave the country for extended periods until she calmed down. Then he saw the rigid muscles of her neck relax, and he let his breath out.

"When I said a handloom," she told him, "I meant a toy."

"Oh. Ah." Thank you, Lord, Ringan thought; her voice was back to normal. "A toy?"

"Sort of; I don't know what to call it. A model, I suppose. A carved wooden representation of a handloom. Which is to say, someone had carved a scale model of a real loom. Which, by the way, Rupert, I know quite well is a massive thing that would take about three lusty boys to shift."

"Don't rub it in, Penny, please. I've already said I was sorry," Ringan said gently. "I'm a bit rattled, you know. Of course you know what a handloom looks like; didn't Candy try her hand at weaving about two years back?"

"She did indeed, and made me that dreadful purple and gold scarf for my birthday, all ratty-tatty homespun, dreadful country chic. I wouldn't have worn it in my own coffin. What a good memory you've got." She sounded admiring, signalling not only her acceptance of Ringan's apology but the offering of an *amende honourable* of her own. As if to prove it, she took up her end of the table again. Ringan wiped his hands on his jeans, hoisted his end, and backed toward the cottage door. They eased the table up the stairs and set it under the round window. It was obvious that they'd found its original setting; the wall showed a faint line where the table's rear edge had long rested.

"Looks a treat, doesn't it?" Penny said. "Well. You've got a settee and two chairs in the parlour, not to mention that game table thing and buffet piece—what is that fancy inlay work called again? Marquetry? Right. And the wrought-iron table thing for the kitchen, but we'll still need stools or chairs or something, especially since you don't like the ones in the barn."

"I'm not having those filthy stools in my kitchen," Ringan said firmly. "Bloody awful things. Vinyl seats! Ugh! Must have been brought in by the army, back around the Coronation. Let's use them for firewood on chilly nights."

". . . so you're fairly set for things. Are we done being longshoremen for the morning? Because if we've gotten as dirty as we're going to get, I'd like a soak."

"Soak on."

Ringan, puttering about downstairs, found himself in a mellow mood. He found an old rag and a tin of lemon and beeswax wood polish. As he cleaned the cherrywood legs of the marquetry game table they'd brought in, he mentally timed the water gurgling into the tub upstairs. Eight minutes. He must remember to ask Pen how far she'd filled the thing . . .

"Hello? Good morning, anyone at home?"

Ringan jumped. He hadn't heard footsteps, or the tapping on his half-opened door. Rag in hand, he stood up and saw Albert Wychsale, with Butterball snaking figure eights between his ankles.

"Good morning," Ringan replied. "Glad you came by. Please, come in. Hello, Butterball, back so soon?"

"Has he already visited? This animal is shameless." Wychsale stepped indoors, casting an appreciative look around. There was an odd look on his face, which Ringan identified as relief, tempered with something else. "My word, you've got the old place looking like a home again. Very nice, very nice indeed, to see Lumbe's taken care of. To tell you the truth, I didn't care to see it standing empty."

"Really?" Ringan was trying to make sense of that look of relief. "Can I offer you a cup of tea?"

"Well, yes, thanks. I was just out for my morning walk. Thought I'd see if you'd found everything, or needed any help." He touched the back of the settee. "Ah, you found the stuff in the barn. I couldn't remember whether I'd told you about it or not. Good to see this stuff back in its proper place." He sniffed deeply. "I remember that smell. Isn't that what you used on the wood up at the House?"

"My private blend. I left some with your housekeeper. Tell her to call me if she runs out, and I'll make up another lot." Wychsale followed Ringan into the kitchen. "I'll just put the kettle on. Cream and sugar?"

"Just cream, please. Looks like you'll need some chairs for this room. Feel free to come up to the House and have a look in the lumber room. There's likely some chairs that would do for this room. Help yourself to what you need."

"Thanks, but I seem to recall that the chairs in the lumber room are high-backed wing chairs from France. It's a nice thought, but I wouldn't have room to move; they're the best part of a meter wide, each. Besides, Chinese dragon-printed red silk brocade, in this kitchen? A bit overwhelming, I'd say." The kettle whistled, and Ringan poured boiling water. "Here you go, white no sugar. All right, Butterball, keep your hair on. I haven't forgotten you. Here's some milk."

"I see he's found another human to spoil him." Wychsale accepted a cup and scratched the cat's head with his free hand. "For a pampered aristocrat, I'd say he's mastered the fine art of begging, wouldn't you?"

"I would. Sit down, Mr. Wychsale. I'm glad you stopped by; we were going to come up and see you later in the day."

"We?"

"My lady friend is upstairs taking a bath. She got a bit dusty helping me unload the barn. What's the matter?"

Wychsale was looking horrified. "There was no need to have a

55

lady help you! You could have asked up to the House. I would have sent down a man to help. I hope she hasn't hurt herself!" At Ringan's involuntary chuckle, he added, a bit stiffly, "Have I said something funny?"

Ringan was grinning. "Only that Penny designs and builds all the stage settings for her theatre troupe. A few bits of furniture won't worry her. She may be a hothouse flower and a toff, but she's not fragile. Still, she does appreciate old-fashioned masculine concern, as long as the concerned males don't get in her way."

" 'Penny'?" Wychsale sipped his tea. "You said a toff, and a theatre troupe? Good heavens, you wouldn't be referring to Penelope Wintercraft-Hawkes by any chance, would you?"

"None other," Ringan said, surprised. "We've been, ah, friends for a long time now, the best part of ten years. Do you know each other? Have you met?"

"No, but I helped sponsor the Summerland Festival two years ago. Her Lady Macbeth was the standout performance of the weekend. A very distinguished lady. The Tamburlaine Players may be the best theatre troupe in England. To tell you the truth, I prefer them to the RSC by a country mile." He sounded animated. "Will she be living here? How nice."

"Afraid not; she has a flat in London. We both travel so much, you see." The compliment to Penny had softened Ringan's mood. "So, you prefer Tamburlaine to the RSC? You'll have to tell Penny that yourself, when she gets out of the bath. She'll be delighted." He caught a sound from upstairs, the first gurgle of bathwater moving through the plumbing, and climbed to his feet. "Sounds like she's finished her soak. Excuse me a moment, will you? She's already come close to losing her temper once today, and coming down wrapped in a towel to find company in the house would definitely put the lid on it."

Penny, stark naked, was drying herself with an old towel of Ringan's when he poked his head through the bathroom door. "Company," he said, in answer to her questioning look. "My noble patron has dropped by to take a shufty at his family's old slave quarters. He's having a cup of tea. By the way, he thinks the Tamburlaine Players blow the RSC out of the water. Oh, and that outfit looks smashing on you."

"But I'm not wearing any . . . Ringan, you lout!" She reached for a comb. "Right, I'll be down in a tick. Keep him occupied."

"Will do." Ringan knew that a long career in rapid costume and makeup changes meant that Penny would waste no time. Sure enough, five minutes later, she came downstairs, fully dressed, hair pulled back in a ponytail, and with a touch of colour on her lips. She paused on the landing, as if preparing for a grand entrance. Ringan, who spotted her first, got a good look at her clothing and bit back a grin. He understood the significance of four hundred quid worth of designer silk quite well. Obviously, she had decided to meet the local aristocracy on her own terms.

"Hullo, darling," she called. Her accent, redolent of her Oxford education, was fractionally more pronounced than usual. She swept regally down the stairs and came forward with a hand outstretched. "Good morning, Mr. Wychsale. It's a pleasure. Oh, I see Ringan's offered you tea. Lovely."

Ringan, controlling twitching lips, took his cue and performed a formal introduction. He met Penny's eye for a second and took a firm grip on his sense of the ridiculous. It would be interesting to see whether the eighth baron responded in form; after all, Penny's family had been landed gentry while William the Conqueror had still been in charge. She was also famous, a Somebody as opposed to a Nobody, not to mention the fact that she was gorgeous.

This fact, at least, was having an obvious impact on Wychsale. In a gesture that sorely tried Ringan's self-control, he took Penny's offered hand and bowed over it, managing a good look at her cleavage before he straightened up again. Penny obligingly gave her shoulders a tiny shrug. The gesture sent her low-cut blouse even farther down.

"Tea, darling? How was your bath?" Ringan was proud of himself; his own voice held barely a tremor. To his delight, Penny winked at him.

"Oh, super! I'd love some tea." *Super?* She never used words like that. Lord, Ringan thought, she was playing the Right Hon like a five-pound trout on a six-pound line. By the time she was done with Wychsale, he'd be offering her the moon, the stars, and probably complete access to his house and lands. Oh, well, she was an actress, after all. He'd best play along with her; certainly he'd never be able to handle Wychsale half as well.

As Ringan poured Penny a cup, snatches of conversation floated through the kitchen door. The Right Honourable was telling Ms. Wintercraft-Hawkes how marvelous her Lady Macbeth was; Ms. Wintercraft-Hawkes was telling Wychsale to do please call her Penny, because being called Penelope made her feel she was back in fourth form again, and really, Wintercraft-Hawkes was such a mouthful, wasn't it? The badinage was as surreal as it was friendly.

Ringan shook his head, bemused. Thank God he was a Celt, not an Anglo. He'd never understand the bloody English if he lived forever, especially the upper classes. They were simply too peculiar. Penny had met Wychsale for the first time four minutes ago. She could care less about Wychsale, and Wychsale surely couldn't be feeling anything stronger than gallantry and the admiration for someone he knew to be good at her craft, yet they were chatting away like each was the other's best friend and last hope of heaven. Were they hypocrites, or was this kiss-kiss pet-pet rubbish inescapable, a part of their social and genetic makeup? Who knew?

". . . always thought tithe barns were built to be enormous," Penny was saying as Ringan came back in with her tea. "Oh, ta, darling. I mean, aren't they called tithe barns because they're supposed to hold a tenth of the harvest?"

"Yes, indeed. What a clever, clever lady." Ringan nearly choked, managed to swallow it, and caught a look of pure mischief from his incorrigible lady love. "You're quite right," Wychsale continued. "Every tenth sheaf of wheat was traditionally stored there for the church. Vast buildings, absolutely vast. Take the Abbey Barn in Glastonbury. A huge stone affair with a crucked roof. It's a typical size for a tithe barn, more like a small cathedral than a barn."

"Really? We must have a look at it later, Ringan." Penny's expression of mild interest didn't waver, but Ringan could see that, for the moment, her attention was caught. "I'm curious, then. Why is that thatched affair in the back garden so small? It's about the size of the cottage. If it was designed to hold so much, shouldn't it be much larger?"

Clever wench, Ringan thought appreciatively. She was getting the information they wanted without arousing the slightest suspicion of anything more than curiosity in the Right Hon's breast. Or were they? There was a peculiar look at the back of Wychsale's eye.

"Ah, I see you've already tumbled to one of our local mysteries." Wychsale set his empty cup down, and Butterball promptly jumped into his lap and began kneading his thighs. "Ouch! Stop it, cat, I'm not a pastry board. The truth is, your barn used to be much larger. In fact, before Lumbe's was built, the barn covered the entire field. It actually extended over the ground the cottage was constructed on."

There was no mistaking Penny's interest now; her eyes gleamed. Why, Ringan wondered, had the information lit a spark? It was time he took a hand in this exchange of information, twisty and indirect though it might be. "Yes," he said thoughtfully. "I seem to remember something about it in the records. A fire, wasn't it?"

"Several fires, actually; the most recent was about a hundred years ago, so nothing recent, but still . . ." Now, why did Wychsale sound so diffident? "That barn has Saxon foundations; the original building was thought to have been a longhouse, presumably used by your basic half-naked savages in rotten sheepskins. Right out of Beowulf. What's the matter?"

"Nothing." Penny swallowed hard, and regained her balance. "So, Ringan was right; it goes back to Saxon times?"

"Yes, indeed, it was put up well before the Conquest. It's burned four separate times, never really completely, but always enough to demand a restructuring, a moving around of the foundation. Every time it was rebuilt, it got smaller. There's a lot of scattered information about the fires in various estate documents. One peculiar thing is that the roof was never really badly damaged, not even in the worst of the fires. My, er, forebears would simply have them take a few planks out between the crucking beams, and shorten it up a length or so. But as to the cause of any of those fires . . ." His voice trailed off.

"Arson?" Penny asked gently. Ringan shot her a quick glance. Wychsale was right, she was clever. She'd zeroed in on that reluctance of his like a cat cornering a mouse.

"No—at least, there's no record of arson ever being suspected." Wychsale abruptly pushed Butterball off his lap. "You'll probably think this is absurd, but the truth is—"

"Glastonbury Tor," Ringan said abruptly. He'd just remembered a few more bits from the records in the Wychsale muniment room. "That was it, wasn't it? There were rumors of black magic, or divine wrath, or maybe some kind of supernatural thing, as a cause of those fires. Because this patch of ground is on a direct ley line with Glastonbury Tor."

"What on earth are you talking about?"

"Ley lines. Geographical lines of mystical power." Ringan turned to Penny. "Local superstition, love, and not just local. The Tor is world-famous as a kind of lightning rod for, well, supernatural disturbances—damn, what's the word I want?"

"A ufocal." Wychsale sounded noncommittal. "Local slang for a focus for unexplained lights in the sky. A sounding board for every wild legend and ghost story you'd ever want to tell on a dark and stormy night. As Ringan says, a lightning rod. One of the legends is that the Tor is the final resting place for King Arthur. Another one says that Merlin the magician is in there, sleeping under a spell or something, although I've heard legends that put him asleep in the heart of Silbury Hill. Of course, this whole area is traditionally associated with Joseph of Arimathea. The thorn tree, the Chalice Well, the Abbey itself. You know?"

"Lord, of course! I actually said something to Ringan about the Abbey looking haunted, just last night. And it's not just Somerset, is it? There's Avebury and Stonehenge in Wiltshire." Penny sounded rueful at her own lapse, but her eyes still gleamed. "It's fascinating, especially if you deal with legend and folklore. Ringan does, all the time, because he's a musician. Isn't this fascinating, Ringan?"

Penny, he thought, you devious thing. Maybe there was something to this torturous, sideways method of extracting information after all. He cleared his throat.

"I do indeed." He picked his words carefully. "And not only as a musician, Pen; it's part of property restoration as well. At least, it is if you go about it the way I do."

"Ringan's very Zen about history," Penny told Wychsale confidingly. "He says there's more to a place's history than its paint and stonework. Oh, but you know that, don't you?"

"To my cost—and to my benefit. That was why I asked Mr. Laine to help me restore Wychsale House. I have a bit of that Zen attitude myself." He saw he'd taken the others aback, and smiled slightly. "Dear me, did I strike you both as stodgy and devoid of imagination? A middle-aged Tory? I'm not, at least not when it comes to my home. I simply don't believe that matching the original wallpaper will bring the spirit of a home back to itself. Take that barn, for example."

"Yes, let's." Penny sounded extremely cordial. "We did wonder about it. Ringan told me how he got Lumbe's and the barn, and it made sense, but the moment we saw that thatched bit of ancient history out there, we were both thrown for a loop. Hadn't you better tell us all about it?"

"Certainly, if you like," Wychsale said blandly. "What do you want to know?"

Penny flapped one hand impatiently. "You've told us, the foundations go back to Edward the Confessor or even before. Ringan saw that at once. And I saw the black streaks on the timbers inside; obviously, there had been a fire. So how did the barn get so small, and so patchwork? Why did they just keep shrinking the place, instead of rebuilding it to its original size? Why did a building that ought to be listed with the National Trust get handed over without a blink? What's the real story behind those mysterious fires? And exactly why does that bloody place feel so—so—"

"Spooky?"

"Spooky," Penny agreed. "We'd really like to know a bit more about the barn's back history, Mr. Wychsale . . ."

"Albert, please. After all, you told me to call you Penny, and Mr. Laine—Ringan—is my neighbor now."

"All right—Albert." Penny suddenly smiled at him, a wide charming smile with no guile at all behind it. "Now, do stop teasing us and tell us about the spooky barn. There must be more to it than legends about the Tor."

"Well, of course there's more. You mean you hadn't guessed?" Wychsale shook his head sadly, and Ringan abruptly realised that Penny wasn't the only expert at this cat-and-mouse game they'd been playing. There had been a flash of amusement in Wychsale's eyes. "And I thought you were so clever. Surely you must have guessed the truth?"

"What in the world are you talking about?" Penny asked sharply. She'd stopped smiling.

"Why, that the barn's haunted, of course. Not a ghost that goes back to Saxon times, but still, a ghost." Wychsale met Ringan's incredulous stare. There was no mistaking the mischief in that look. "A tragic young ghost, too, if the admittedly scattered reports of the haunting are true. I'm surprised you haven't seen him. Isn't that what, ah, piqued your interest?"

For a moment Penny and Ringan gaped at him. Ringan was aware of Penny's dropped jaw, and with a certain detached interest wondered if her incredulity was touched with resentment at having been outduelled by a master. After all, she'd been using every ounce of well-bred English charm she possessed to weasel information out of the Right Hon. Now it seemed that the Right Hon had known it all along, and he'd been amusing himself by playing along with her. For the life of him, Ringan couldn't help grinning. He caught Penny's eye, saw her face crinkle up, and began to chuckle.

Penny's gale of laughter broke the remaining ice and shattered the artificial formality of the conversation. She abandoned the pose with regret. "Somerset one, Gloucester nil," she told Wychsale, and wiped her streaming eyes. "Gloucester resigns gracefully, having been beaten on all points. Game over. Please do tell us what you can, Albert. I had a very bizarre experience in the barn this morning, and I've never been psychic or anything like it, and I'm simply dying to know more about it, and so is Ringan. Aren't you, Ringan?"

Ringan, who'd been silently asking his Celtic gods to preserve him from the wiles of the bloody Sassenach, nodded at Wychsale. What the hell, information was information. If it saved him hours of time-consuming research, he might as well take it any way it was offered.

"It would be my pleasure, at least as much as I know, which honestly isn't much," Wychsale told them, and stood up. "But unfortunately, I can't do it this morning. I've got a meeting with my banker in about twenty minutes. I'd only planned to drop in and see that Ringan had got moved in all right. If you'd like to come up to the House for dinner tonight, we can discuss it over drinks. About seven? I'm keeping early hours at the moment; there's estate work that needs my attention."

"We'll be there," Penny told him. "Before you rush off, Albert, let me ask you one thing. Was this house used by the army at all during the Second World War?"

"Somerset Light Infantry." Wychsale seemed unsurprised by this non sequitur. "From 1943 until right after V-E Day. I was still in rompers back then. Did you want to talk to them? Most of them are dead now, of course, but I can put you in touch with someone who was here then. He was a raw recruit back then, barely seventeen, I'd say. His name's Jack Calder. Interested?"

"Very." Ringan was scrabbling for a pen and paper. "Do you have his number?"

"You won't need it." Wychsale paused with one hand on the doorknob. "He's one of my gardeners; very elderly now, of course, but he likes to put in a few hours a day in the field. He says it helps keep him fit. He likes the extra money, too. A pension doesn't get you what it once did, you know? I'll send him down now, if you like."

"That was a time. Dog days of the war, you might say, with bloody Hitler and his buzzards rampaging all over Europe like a plague of locusts. And no one knowing how it would go, no one at all. Leastways, if anyone knew, they weren't telling us. This is good beer, Mr. Laine, very good indeed. Working the fields is a thirsty business."

Jack Calder wiped a hand over his mouth, as if hoping to catch a few stray flecks of tasty foam. He was a small man in his early eighties, with bright blue eyes and an enviable thatch of iron-gray hair. He boasted the healthy skin of the true countryman; it didn't take much, Ringan thought, to see that the retired military man had largely avoided the stress and pollution of the big cities.

Penny, who'd played high society with Wychsale, had reverted to her normal self for Calder. She'd changed into jeans, put together a pile of thick, salty ham sandwiches, and applauded Ringan's percipience in purchasing a dozen bottles of the local brew the previous night. Tea, she said, was for the nobs. A man who'd been working the fields since sunup would prefer beer. "There's more beer, if you'd fancy it," she urged the old man. "And have another sandwich, do."

"I'll wait a bit on the sandwiches, miss, if you don't mind. I wouldn't say no to another beer, though."

Ringan passed him a bottle. "So you actually worked in this cottage during the war. How long was that for?"

"Two years, give a bit. I was just turned eighteen, and green as they come." The blue eyes were clear and unsentimental. "And I was right lucky to be stationed close to home, let me tell you. My mum was sickly, and my sister too young to cope. She was fifteen, helping with the evacuees up at the big house. I had it easy enough, being able to go home at night and see that all was well with them."

"You were lucky," Penny agreed soberly. "Did your family live in Glastonbury?"

"Over to Shepton Mallet. Close enough, you might say."

"How did you get stationed so close to home?" Ringan found himself strongly drawn to the old man; there was an honesty to him, a complete lack of frill, that was pleasing. "You said your mother wasn't well. Was that it?"

"No, though it's true she was a cripple." No political correctness here; Calder believed in calling a spade a spade. "It was because I knew a fair bit about communications, you see. Radio waves and the like. Also, I was good at codes, what they call cryptography. The southern counties were dotted all over with communications posts."

"I suppose it makes sense," Penny said thoughtfully. "Glastonbury is just far enough from the coast not to be a prime target, but close enough to monitor what was going on. I suppose it was all very hush-hush?"

"Aye, it was," Calder agreed. "Everyone had one eye over their shoulders, all the time. Fifth columnists and the like, and them Mosley people. Hard to believe, isn't it?"

Ringan understood the old man's meaning. "That anyone could have seen what Hitler was doing, and still supported him? Too right it's hard to believe. But tell us about your time here, Mr. Calder. What was the barn used for?"

"Storage, mostly." Calder drained his remaining beer. The clear blue eyes had suddenly become guarded. "Communications equipment, transmitters. And blankets. We always seemed to be short of blankets in those days."

"You needn't get too specific if it worries you." Penny had caught that guarded look. "I don't suppose it matters, not after all this time, and it isn't really the military information we're looking for anyway."

"Oh, that's not worrying me. I don't suppose either of you was born for a good many years after the war. But I have some right strange memories of this cottage, and some even stranger ones of that barn out there."

Penny flashed Ringan a warning glance. "Well," she said, "that's a coincidence. We've been here one day, and we already have a couple of right strange memories of our own. Would it worry you to tell us about yours?"

Calder was quiet for so long that Ringan thought the old man was going to refuse. Then he realised that Calder, a careful man to the core, was merely choosing his words.

"No," he said slowly, "it wouldn't worry me. Likely I'm foolish, worrying about it now. After all, I've spent close on fifty years working these fields, knowing what I knew about Lumbe's Cottage and the old barn the whole time. But I can remember how I felt, back then. It's a strange thing. So much to remember, so many years gone by. But that feeling I had, when I first walked into the barn, that's the clearest memory I've got. Sixty years, and I can still close my eyes and it comes up in me like a spring tide." He shook his head and looked from Penny to Ringan, almost pleadingly. "Don't make any sense, does it? But that's the way of it."

"I know just how you feel." Ringan thought back to that stab of cold he'd felt, that indistinct brush against his back, that half-heard sigh. It was easy to believe that if he made it to Calder's age, he'd still be able to call up that incredulous sense of fear and sorrow in all its dark clarity. "Did anything happen to you here, in Lumbe's proper? Or was it just in the barn?"

"All in the barn, Mr. Laine. But that's not to say there wasn't them who left this cottage with a few sleepless nights in their future, and right glad they were to be going when they got demobbed. Oliphant, for one, and Winlit. Oh, they couldn't shake the dust of Lumbe's from their heels fast enough, once the war was over. We never discussed it, but I knew, right enough."

"Oliphant? Winlit? Were they mates of yours?"

"In a manner of speaking, miss, though really just a meal together sometimes and taking in a picture at the cinema in Street. Folks are thrown together in wartime, otherwise I'd not have bothered. They were foreigners, you know, from the North." There was a ghostly echo of an old, indulgent scorn in the old man's voice. "Manchester, I think it was. Not from these parts, anyway."

Ringan's lips twitched at this parochialism. "Well, I'm a foreigner from the North myself, you know, Mr. Calder. Scotland, I think it was."

"That you are not, Mr. Laine. No foreigner could have done up the big house that way, not without knowing in his bones how we do things in Somerset. Wouldn't matter if you came from China; anyone around here would shake your hand and know you were one of our own."

"Ta for that." Ringan, oddly moved, cleared his throat. "What happened in the barn, Mr. Calder?"

"Aye, I'd best tell you, hadn't I? After all, it's what I came to do." Jack Calder took a deep breath, settled himself firmly on the sofa, and began his tale of an autumn day in 1943.

Nineteen forty-three had, indeed, been the dog days of the Second World War. The frenzy of the Blitzkrieg and the will-we-or-won't-we lull of earlier years seemed unreal. France had fallen, and Belgium, and Norway. The universe had become news bites in the headlines, redefining itself as lines of attack and retreat; the Vistula line, the Maginot line. It was tragic, and unavoidable, and exhausting.

If the news was to be believed, events were moving badly for the fascists. During the winter of the previous year, Hitler had committed a supreme piece of military idiocy and charged into the deepest bowels of Russia. Ill-equipped, his supply factories destroyed by Allied bombers, up against some of the fiercest and most romantic soldiers on earth when it came to invaders on their home soil, the fascists had lost over half a million men during three months of fighting in the brutal Russian winter.

In the meantime, the Allied forces had been busy all over the European theatre, invading Sicily in July of 1943, after having taken back Africa from Mussolini in the warm days of May. What was going on in the Pacific theatre was far enough away from England's green and pleasant land to seem like the events on another planet.

The tide was turning at last. But at home in England, there was numbness, weariness, a sense that this damned thing had been going on forever and might never end. Across the Channel, France and Belgium were still firmly held by Hitler. The wounds from the Luftwaffe's destruction of Coventry, the blitzes of London that had left more than fourteen thousand civilians dead in the rubble, were dull omnipresent aches.

Jack Calder, at twenty years old, was already something of a veteran. A talent for anything to do with communications systems or codes had rendered him valuable enough to those in charge to put him above the ranking of cannon fodder. He'd joined the army the moment he'd reached legal age, expecting to see some basic training before being shipped off to Italy or Africa. Instead he'd been stationed two miles from home, a fact that pleased his family more than it had pleased him. He was, at the time, a romantic boy still young enough to find the notion of death on the battlefield an honourable ending.

He'd been aware of the Wychsale estate and family since birth, of course. Somerset is a small place, a series of small towns clustered around minor cities. The system went back to Saxon times. Where the church had built its diocesan centres, the towns had grown to importance and economic stature, while smaller towns and villages acted as satellites and sources of income. Glastonbury, with its huge abbey, had been the area's economic and spiritual heart for time out of mind. If, in the twentieth century, it was no longer of great importance, there was no one to convince the locals of that fact. The Wychsales had stood as lords of the manor since the Tudors took power, and local lords they remained. Jack Calder, born and reared within sighting distance of the Abbey, knew all about the Wychsales.

Jack's father had himself served with the Somerset Light Infantry during the Great War, and Jack thought it only right that he do the same. Everyone did their part for the war effort; men fought, women drove ambulances and did whatever they could. Richard Albert St. John Wychsale, forty years old and lord of the manor, was himself a major with the RAF. Jack's sister Mary, helping at the evacuee center at Wychsale House, had kind words for Mrs. Wychsale and the boy, Albert, at that time an energetic child of four.

Still, Jack had never set foot on Wychsale property until the day he was stationed at the communications post for western Somerset. After his experience in the tithe barn, he was so shaken that Africa or Italy would have seemed like a holiday.

Lumbe's itself smelled of paint and dust; the army had installed modern wiring, as well as a new water heater and telephone lines.

The cottage had been empty for ten years, since Peter Wychsale, maimed and crippled during the Boer War, had finally died in his bed.

It was because of Peter's invalidism that the upper story had been added. He had been a splendid physical specimen when he left for Pretoria. Capture by a Boer troop during the Ladysmith action had resulted in ten ugly days of brutal torture. By the time the Boer position was overtaken, he'd been near death and crippled beyond all fixing, his bones twisted, his back hunched. Sent home after a long stay at a British army hospital, his family—mother, father, and young brother Richard—had found him changed in more than body. The open, idealistic boy of twenty had become a bitter, reclusive man.

His mother had given him what he needed most: privacy. She had insisted that her husband fix the old cottage, empty for decades, to give the invalid every comfort possible. So Lumbe's gained a proper indoor bathroom and loo, and two bedrooms. It had then gained two residents, Peter and the middle-aged batman who had been his servant for every moment of eight years, except for ten bad days in South Africa.

The batman had died in '27, and had been replaced by another retired military man. Peter himself had finally died at age fifty-five, living longer than anyone expected. His brother Richard, still a bachelor and younger by twenty years, came into the estate. Since he'd always known he would, he was therefore prepared. He married in '38, begot a son, and proved his competence as lord of the manor. Under his stewardship, the Wychsale holdings had actually grown.

Richard, too young for the Great War, was past forty when the Second World War broke out. Still, he did his part; if his ranking as an RAF major involved more paperwork than it did dogfighting, he performed well. He was an able administrator, and a fierce patriot; above all, he was that rarity, a wealthy humanist. When the army wanted Lumbe's for a communications post, he made the arrangements with the Somerset Light Infantry. He also offered Wychsale House as a home for evacuees. His wife Margaret, a strong-minded woman, came up with the notion of using it as a hospital as well.

The staff at Lumbe's consisted of five men; two officers and three men under them. Jack was the youngest; knowing that Winlit and Oliphant were his seniors in age, Jack had expected to be treated like an afterthought. He was surprised to find himself mistaken, and didn't know that his own attitude toward them was touched with superiority. After all, he and the officers were local men; Winlit and Oliphant were not. Since he was unaware that this attitude showed, he mislabeled their respect as friendliness, a misconception that worked out well for all concerned.

His first three days were spent learning the layout of the grounds, familiarizing himself with the sensitive equipment, and acquainting himself with his fellows. On the fourth day, he walked into Lumbe's to find Winlit on his knees on the parlour floor. He was surrounded by a complex welter of wires, knobs, and tubes. He was also swearing fluently under his breath.

"Problems?" Jack asked genially. He had eaten a hot breakfast and drunk two cups of tea; his mother seemed better that morning than she'd seemed in a while. The world looked brighter than usual, and his mood was cheerful.

"Bloody wires," Winlit said morosely. "Three of them, all broken. I wish the boys in the back room would check their tats and bobs before they send the stuff down to us."

"Know what you mean, mate." Jack squatted beside him, peering at the half-assembled device. "What have we got here? Looks like radar, only it's too small."

"It's radar, all right. New portable casing, made just for us noncoms out in the wilds. Supposed to make it easy for us to track the jerries. Problem is, the wires." Winlit cast a look over his shoulder, making sure neither of his superior officers had arrived. Reassured, he stood and gave the pile a light kick with one toe. "Sometimes I wonder if these London geniuses could build a bootlace that didn't break first time out."

"Well look, Tommy, don't worry about it. There's a length of this stuff out in the barn. I'll pop out and cut you some, and rig it up as well. Here, let's measure it."

"Ta, mate." Winlit was honestly grateful. "I'd go myself, only I'm supposed to mind the store till the others get here. Anyway . . ."

"Anyway, I know where it's kept and you don't. Not to worry. Back in a tick."

Every staff member had a key to Lumbe's, but only the two officers and Jack had a key to the shiny new padlock on the barn. This was Jack's third trip into the barn. The first had been a mere glance through the doors; the second had been spent organising the stores and supplies. He'd been too busy that day to do more than what his job required.

He noticed this morning, though. From the moment he laid a hand to the padlock, he noticed.

He was not particularly sensitive; sensitivity is not a luxury a hardworking countryman can afford. But he'd have to have been dead not to have felt it; a stillness, a hush. It felt, Jack told his hosts sixty years later, as if the very ground beneath the barn were holding its breath.

Jack Calder, dimly amazed at himself, found that he really, truly, did not want to enter that barn.

He tried to get hold of himself. There was a war on, and wire to be cut, and anyway, he told himself firmly, he was being right daft. What in hell was he doing, standing about shivering in his own sweat, like a bloody puppy in a rainstorm? Anyone would think he was walking into a chamber of horrors, like that story of the Princess Elizabeth sitting on the Traitors Gate steps because she didn't want to walk into the Tower of London. He wasn't a Royal, and this wasn't the Tower; it was just an old barn that he'd been in before. None of this altered the fact that the thought of turning the key in the padlock made him flinch, and the idea of pushing the door open made him weak in the knees.

He argued with himself, he chastised himself. After a few minutes of this, he ran out of arguments and listened to the silence, the hush, the sense of being a fly who knew, just knew, that beyond the barn door was a hungry spider with a vast web . . .

Then, into that silence, had came voices.

"Voices?" Penny asked sharply. "Do you mean singing?"

"No." Jack raised a fresh bottle of beer to his lips and tipped the contents down his throat. He was clammy with the fear-sweat of more than half a century ago. "Speaking. A man and a woman. I couldn't hear words, you understand? Just—tones. He sounded normal enough. She sounded different, though. Worried, upset, something. Raised the hair on the back of my neck, it did. I stood and listened and sometimes I thought she'd break out crying, and then she wouldn't. I heard him laugh, once. Not mean, just a laugh. I nearly pissed myself." He caught himself and cast an apologetic look at Penny. "Voices. Inside the barn, all locked up."

"God," Ringan said simply. "Scary. What did you do?"

What Jack Calder had done, after swallowing convulsively, was twist the key in the padlock, push the doors open, and walk into the barn.

"What!" Penny stared at the old man. "You—you hero!"

If she'd expected modesty, she got none. "Aye, I was all of that," he agreed. "At least, that's what I think now. Mind you, I'd not do it today, not for anything you could offer me. But I went in. My heart was going like a runaway horse, my legs were like jelly-bags, I was cold as a corpse, and all the hair on my head wanted to stand straight up and salute, but I was young and stupid and in the army. So I went in."

Ringan found that every hair on his own body was alive with sympathetic static. "What—did you see anything?"

"See? No, not really—just a kind of sparkly bit on the floor, as if some light had gotten in from somewhere and was lying about. If it's anything really strange you're meaning, no, nothing. Only the supplies, all neat and tidy, the way I'd arranged them. But I thought I heard crying, a woman's voice crying, dying out to a whisper. And the sound of water, running water. Very loud, it was. And there was a smell." Jack Calder's bright old eyes were fixed on a past, somewhere in the distance between his hosts. "They say smell is the sense that brings back old times the most, don't they? The experts, I mean. Too right. To this day I can't smell the stuff without that morning coming back to me."

"What was it you smelled?" Penny asked. The question was unnecessary; she already knew.

"Lavender," Jack Calder said simply. "Soft and sweet, like a perfume in a lady's hair. Lavender."

Five

I went to my love's bedroom door
Where often times I had been before
But I could not speak nor yet get in
The pleasant bed that my love lies in.

"Ringan Laine's residence."

"Penny?" The voice crackled down the line. "Oh Lord, please be Penny, or else I've dropped a horrible brick."

"Jane?" Penny motioned at Ringan, poised at the door. "I haven't seen you in ages. How are you?"

"Oh, good, it *is* you. It only just occurred to me that Ringan might have gone utterly out of character and slipped a bit of fluff in on the side." Jane Castle sounded grateful, before it occurred to her that Penny might well have grounds to take her suggestion the wrong way. She promptly lost herself in a tangled morass of attempted explanations. "I don't mean Ringan goes in for that, of course not, but, well, you know, new home and you might not have been there, I suppose it would be only natural if he celebrated by— oh, God. Shut *up*, Jane. What in heaven's name am I going on about?"

"I haven't a clue, but not to worry." Penny was grinning Ringan, who'd come up and was pointing ostentatiously at his watch, raised his eyebrows. "Here's Ringan, Jane."

"Jane? What's up?" He took the phone from Penny's out-stretched hand and listened for a moment. "You're in Plymouth? Yes, of course you can, but—oh, tomorrow night? Sure, we'd love to see you. Call me when you get into Glastonbury, I'll give you directions then. Right now we're late for dinner with the Right Honourable Albert Wychsale."

The phone crackled again, this time with emphasis.

"No, I haven't gone all upscale and county on you, and I'm not crawling into bed with the aristos, not unless you mean Penny, and if you do I think you're being bloody rude. Look, love, can I tell you about it tomorrow? We're really going to be late for dinner. Ta, bye."

"Your first real guest. How nice." Penny followed him out into the warm spring evening. "What's she doing in Plymouth, of all places?"

"Did you hear me ask?" They strolled out to Penny's car. She'd wanted him to drive, but he'd been adamant; when she saw Wychsale House, she'd understand why the Jaguar fit the prevailing decor better than his slightly battered little Alfa. And since no one on earth drove Penny's Jaguar but Penny, she was behind the wheel. "What do you mean, my first real guest? What are you, then?"

"Oh, I'm just your upscale, aristo bit of fluff. And if you dare to call me a guest . . ."

"No, no," he said hastily. "Wouldn't dream of it. I like that dress, by the way. Is it supposed to fit you like a second skin? You look smashing tonight."

"I'd better," she said cheerfully. "You simply don't want to know what this bit of Armani cost."

"You're probably right, and I won't ask why you saw fit to drag an Armani into the wilds of Somerset. You doubtless have your reasons, and I'm not quibbling with the results." He leaned back against the leather seat as Penny started the car. It occurred to him that she drove with the same easy proficiency that marked her every skill, and he told her so.

"Silver-tongued devil, you are." She turned the car onto the road. "Hmmmm. If you like the Armani, wait till you see what else I've got packed. I was too knackered to model it last night, but I will later."

"Sounds dangerous. A little something?"

"More little than something. Designed to drive my lover into a screaming frenzy, or so said the saleswoman at my favourite chichi overpriced shop in Knightsbridge, when I tried it on."

"Really?" Ringan said appreciatively. "A screaming frenzy? How nice for me. I can hardly wait."

"You'll have to. We don't want the Right Hon to have an apoplexy and go down face first into his crème brûlée, do we now? Which way do I turn, Ringan? My God, these roads are dark!"

"Left, and left again at the next crossroads. There, see those lights up ahead? About a half mile down the road, onto a wide drive with two stone gryphons at the end of it, and Bob's your uncle."

"Good, because I'm starving. Tell me," she said, with no change in her voice, "what did you think of Jack Calder's memoirs this afternoon?"

"I thought he was telling the truth, at least as he remembered it. I don't think he's even capable of guile, Penny; I doubt I've ever met anyone so transparently honest. And there was that mention of lavender."

"There was, indeed." She pulled the car to a stop and waited for Ringan to get out and open her door. The behavior was ingrained; in a social situation of this kind, she would act the great lady until hell froze over. It was a learned reaction, and detracted not at all from her own fierce brand of independence. He obliged her, and led her up the wide, shallow front steps to the door of the house.

Wychsale himself ushered them in, blinking as he got an eyeful of Penny's dress, and accepting their offering of wine with thanks. Glancing around the hall, Penny took in the original William Morris wallpaper, the paintings, the delicate molding in the cornices. She caught Ringan's eye, and a wordless message passed between them. He'd been right; her Jag was just the thing to grace the front drive of this exquisite period piece. In fact, it was rather a pity neither of them owned a vintage Bentley.

Wychsale offered cocktails, was refused with thanks, and seemed relieved. "We'll be eating in the morning room," he told them, leading the way. "I'd forgotten that my cook would be away this evening, so we'll have pot luck, something informal." He glanced at Penny's dress again, this time doubtfully. "I do hope you don't mind."

"I think we'd prefer it, actually." Ringan smiled at him. "Your dining room is a bit oversized for just two guests." He turned to Penny. "It seats twenty-six, and that's before the leaves are added to the table."

"I'm not surprised in the least," she said cryptically. "The morning room let it be. What a gorgeous house. Very orderly, nicely planned, I mean. Nicely laid out."

"Thank you." Wychsale seemed pleased. "I'd give you the grand tour, but it looks better in daylight. Actually, Ringan should do it; he knows more about the history of it than I do."

"Speaking of history," Ringan said as they seated themselves at a small oval table with cabriole legs, "I wanted to thank you for letting Jack Calder spend some time with us today. He was very, um, enlightening. Oh, that smells good. What is it?"

"I believe it's called Italian salad. My cook tells me it's basically chicken, with some rather esoteric vegetables thrown in, and quite a bit of garlic. Also, there's a bit of sauce; the cook is French-trained, I'm afraid, and has rather a thing for sauces. May I give you some, Penny? There's a bottle of California chablis in the cooler. I'm glad Calder was able to help you. Did he clear up any mysteries?"

"Actually, he did." Ringan sampled the chicken. "Mmm. Sauce, indeed, and very tasty it is, too. According to Jack, he hadn't been at Lumbe's a week before he had a close encounter in the barn. Something similar to what happened to Penny this morning."

"Interesting." Wychsale cocked an eyebrow. "But, if you recall, I wasn't able to stay long enough to get the story from you this morning. What happened to Penny?"

Ringan waved his fork at Penny. "Over to you, love."

Penny swallowed a mouthful of salad, took a sip of wine to clear her throat, and gave Wychsale a concise account of everything that had happened since the previous day. As a summary of events, it was logical, orderly, and convincing. It occurred to Ringan that she'd been marshalling her thoughts for just this purpose, and when she had done, he added details of his own experiences, both in the barn and on the stairs. Of his own deepening unease at Penny's dislocated reactions to the proximity of ghosts, he said nothing; this was neither the time nor the place.

Wychsale listened without interruption, and with an impassive face, but his eyebrows betrayed him. By the time Ringan finished, they'd puckered into a vee. He nodded, and turned to Ringan.

"Cold," he said unexpectedly. "You said you felt cold, on the stairwell. Cold, and weak. Yes?"

"Yes." The morning room was warm, and brightly lit. Yet a chilly ripple moved over Ringan's shoulders. "It was right royally nasty, let me tell you."

"You don't have to tell me. I already know." Wychsale had seen that shudder. "Believe me, I know. But I hadn't realised that it worked on adults."

His guests looked at each other. "Would you please be an angel," Penny said carefully, "and explain that?"

"The cold." There was something in Wychsale's eyes that reflected a very different man from the genially fussy aristocrat Ringan had grown used to. "It happened to me, Ringan, in just the same spot you say it happened to you. That was a long time ago, and I've been past the front door of Lumbe's since then, many times, but it's never happened again. I never heard of anyone else having that experience in the house itself. So I thought that it, whatever it is, only bothered itself with children. From what you've just told me, I was wrong."

"How old were you?" Penny asked quietly. She seemed to follow this not very coherent explanation easily enough.

"Six, possibly seven. Quite young." Wychsale abruptly drained his wineglass. "It was in the last days of the war, right around the time of V-E Day. The army had moved out, and I thought they might have left some interesting tats and bobs I could help myself to."

"Ah, the exploration of Ali Baba's treasure cave," Ringan said appreciatively. "I'd have done the same, because who could possibly resist? What were you hoping to find? Bits of equipment, radios, electronic gear you could take apart and put back together again?"

"All of that, and who knows what else. My father wasn't too keen on the idea; in fact, he'd forbidden me straight out to play around the cottage." He looked at them appealingly, in a mute request for their understanding. "But you know how it is at that age; the moment someone tells you not to do something, you get completely obsessed with doing it."

"In through the out door." Ringan nodded. "Lumbe's is quite a distance from the House. How did you get there?"

"Oh, I spent a lot of time out on the estate with the workers. My father was a younger son, you know? His older brother Peter had been maimed past repair during the Boer War. When it became obvious that my father would inherit, he threw himself into learning every aspect of that inheritance, and he made very sure I did the same. He was always sending me out to see how crops were handled, or livestock rotated, or some such thing. I learned quite a bit that way."

"He sounds like a wise man," Penny said dreamily. She was turning her long-stemmed glass between her fingers, watching the pale wine catch reflections from the light. "And I expect it was very good fun, as well. I used to attach myself to the field hands during school holidays, when I was a child back at Whistler's Croft. I watched a family of rabbits getting born. It was amazing. So you hitched a ride with some of the field hands did you? And fetched up at Lumbe's."

"As you say." Wychsale, too, was focussing on Penny's wineglass. There was something soothing about her rhythmic turning of the crystal. "I came down with the chaps who'd been sent to prune the apple trees. It was a blustery day, with a simply huge sky, the kind you don't get in a city. All hurrying clouds and talking wind. You know?"

The verbal picture was vivid, and his guests, both country-bred, nodded. Satisfied, Wychsale continued. "I remember I did my bit, asked some bright questions, picked up a few windfalls. They were all over the ground there, even bobbing about in the stream. As I said, a windy day. I stuffed a few of the less wormy-looking ones into my pockets, waited until the men were busy with their ropes and saws and shears, and slipped across the bridge, right to Lumbe's back door."

"Bridge?" Ringan asked sharply. "What bridge? I don't remember seeing one near the cottage."

"Oh, it's gone now; the floods in 'fifty-eight washed it away. It was very old, two hundred years at the least, and one of the supports had rotted and weakened. It collapsed when the stream burst its banks. There's a new one to replace it, a good half mile farther upstream. But back in 'forty-six, the old bridge was still there."

"Right. So what happened?"

"Well, the first thing I did was to have a hunt round for the keys." A reluctant grin flickered in Wychsale's eyes. "Which, as it turned out, was a waste of time. The cottage wasn't locked."

"Wasn't it?" Penny asked, startled. "Now, that does surprise me. I'd expect the military boys to have been a bit more careful with someone else's property, especially when they'd been lent it."

"It surprised me too. After all, Daddy had given me an earful about sensitive expensive equipment, and government property, and the like. I remember when I pushed that door and it swung open, I was quite cross about it."

"Who were you cross at?" Ringan grinned at him. "Your dad for the lecture, or the army for being careless?"

"Who knows, at that age? Probably both. The point was, you see, that the door's being unlocked convinced me that there was no justification at all for not going in and exploring to my heart's content. And that is just what I proceeded to do."

"Did you find anything?"

"Nothing. Not a notepad, not a fuse, not a crowbar or a plug or a pin. They'd tidied up, all right. They'd even washed the windows before they left. Very disappointing. So, by way of rebellion, I decided to have a look upstairs. I'd never been there before that day, you see."

"Never?" Penny pursed her lips. "Really never? Why not?"

"Well, my uncle died before I was born, so Lumbe's was unoccupied. By the time I was old enough to notice the place or care, Dad had handed it over to the Somerset Light Infantry boys, and they'd fixed things up with Intelligence. I was only just old enough to be aware of it, and the first thing I was told was that it was off-limits. Why do you think I was so fascinated?"

"Bluebeard's chamber. Aha!" Ringan regarded his host with a kindly eye; as he later explained to Penny, there was something quite humanising about envisioning the Right Hon as Baby Bertie. "So you crept up the stairs, in search of treasure or a row of severed heads or something. Did you find anything?"

"I never made it all the way up." Wychsale's gaze had retreated again, fixing itself upon a long-gone moment. "I wasn't allowed to. Something on the stairs stopped me."

No one said anything. Something, perhaps a remembered horror, had settled on Wychsale. It was there in the set of his shoulders, his clenched fingers, the bead of sweat that appeared from nowhere along his unobtrusively retreating hairline. Penny and Ringan glanced at each other, each feeling that the charming room held unpleasant echoes.

The silence held a moment too long for Ringan. "What I felt, was it? Cold like a slap in the face, or a hard kick between your shoulder blades? Almost as if whatever it was had been waiting there, just for you?"

"I hadn't meant to do anything wrong." Wychsale seemed to be talking to himself, or to someone long gone. Certainly he was, at that moment, unaware of his guests. His voice was barely a whisper, and his small mouth was pursed as though he might suddenly burst into tears. It was horrible to see. "Really I hadn't. I'd gone halfway up the stairs and stood there, thinking, you know, and catching my breath. There was sun coming through the window, light all rosy-coloured and warm, light that was moving around because of those wind-driven clouds. All I did was stop on the stairs."

"Albert," Penny said urgently, and her voice was cracked and frightened. "Albert!"

She might not have spoken at all. "And then it hit me, like a wolf coming out from between the trees in a fairy story. Cold, so cold, like something dying. That's what it was, like someone dying, holding on to me with both hands as if by touching me it could keep from dying, or maybe drag me into dying right along with it. And I could feel breathing on me, something moving across me. Like something dying was crawling all over me . . ."

"Did you cry?"

Ringan's voice, deliberate and blightingly matter-of-fact, jerked Wychsale back to himself as Penny's terrified appeal had not. He shook himself once, like a swimmer coming out of deep water. After a moment, his eyes cleared.

"No." His voice sounded rusty. "All I did was to make sickly little whimpering sounds. I was far too frightened to move, and too weak, and most of all I was too overwhelmed. I clung to that banister as if it linked my soul to my body, and forced myself to concentrate on that patch of rose-coloured light on the landing floor. After a bit it all came back to normal. Even the smell faded. And then I picked myself up off my frightened-witless little bottom and fled outdoors as fast as my legs would carry me."

"I don't remember any smell. What was it?" Even as he asked, Ringan knew what Wychsale would say. The knowledge was in Penny's face, as well. There could be only one answer, and Wychsale gave it.

"Lavender," he said simply. "It was on my hands, too, a faint sweet scent. Took three days to fade. That's why I said I thought something was touching me. Well, something must have, mustn't it? Because by the time I turned and ran down the stairs, the smell was already gone out of the air. But it was on my hands. Even my nanny noticed. She was furious because she thought I'd got into her precious cache of pre-war French soap."

"If you want to know what I think," Ringan said from the Jag's passenger seat, "I think things are coming a bit clearer."

"I couldn't agree more." Penny shifted down a gear and negotiated a tricky turn. "Lavender. That says a woman. I bet it's that Betsy bird. The weaver's light-o-love."

"She must have died there, in the house, and I'll bet you it wasn't a natural death. After all, you don't get a haunting this thorough without some kind of tragedy, some kind of cataclysm. Or at least that's what every ghost story I've ever read seems to think—supposedly, a violent death ties you to the spot where you die, if you happen to be a ghost. Careful, here's the turn."

"I see it, ta ever so." Penny turned, drove another thirty yards, and pulled the car off the road and onto Lumbe's front drive. She killed the engine, but showed no immediate inclination to get out. "Interesting that the cold hits on the stairwell, isn't it? Because, if it was this Betsy woman, then the timing's all wrong. Her boyfriend was in Waterloo-era homespuns. And Albert says there weren't any stairs for nearly a century after that."

"There weren't. I had a quick look at Lumbe's records in his muniment room, when I decided to take the place on. The first floor was added when Bertie's Uncle Peter came home from South Africa, all cocked up. And if our indoor visitor is a woman, any woman at all, she predates the upstairs. No woman has lived there since that level was added. Apparently, Uncle Peter was a bitter old recluse, and the only person he allowed in the house was his old batman from the wars, and later on, another old military chap to carry him to the loo and bring him his meals. But I doubt he'd even have had a woman in the house as a guest."

Penny pushed the car door open. "So tomorrow we go and look at the records for the early nineteenth century?"

"We do indeed," Ringan told her, following her up the path. "And we hope like mad that the Wychsale records have what we need. Otherwise, it's going to mean some long hours spent hunting up local newspaper reports in a lot of dusty old archives in Glastonbury's library, and frankly I'd rather be trying to bring up the finish on all this poor neglected furniture, or working in the garden . . ."

". . . or playing Lord Randall with the best traditional flutist on earth," Penny finished, watching him unlock the cottage door. "Remember, Jane's due in tomorrow."

"That's right, I'd forgotten." Ringan pushed the door open and flicked the lights on. "I wonder if she'll pick up on either of our resident uninviteds," he said thoughtfully. "Probably she will, now I think about it. I mean, our ghosts don't seem too selective about who they complain to. I must remember to warn her. A face full of ectoplasm would make her quite cross."

Penny laughed. The cottage looked warm and inviting, the old bricks gleaming dully, every wooden surface showing a fine patina, brought up by Ringan's earlier work with his special polish. She dropped her purse on the marquetry table and stretched, watching Ringan through narrowed eyes.

Out of nowhere, a lusty, sensual mood took her in its hold; she felt suddenly that what she really wanted to do was to drag him up the stairs and throw him on the bed. Looking at him as he leaned against the kitchen door, she saw her exact thought reflected in his face, from the gleam in his eyes to the sudden bristling of his beard. For a full minute they stared at each other, neither saying a word.

Ringan spoke first, his voice wicked and husky. "Didn't you say you'd brought something with you? Something I'd like even better than the Armani? Guaranteed to drive me into a screaming frenzy?"

"More little than something," Penny agreed, and laughed, a deep, throaty sound that, by itself, had been enough to drive Ringan into a screaming frenzy for years. "Shall I put it on? Model it for you?"

"Only if you don't mind me tearing it off you again." He felt himself twitch, quiver, not quite settle. This was two nights running he'd been unable to keep his hands off her. At his age, and after so long a relationship, this was surely something to approve of. Either the cottage air had an aphrodisiac quality, or else he'd been missing her more than he'd realised. "Do you mind that?"

"Not at all." Her pupils seemed unable to decide whether they wanted to be black holes or pinpricks, and a deep, warm flush mantled her shoulders. "I'll just go up and get changed. Give me five and then come up. Yes?"

"Yes, indeed, lady. Yes indeed."

Considering how aroused he was, Ringan spent the next five minutes displaying quite remarkable good sense. He locked the doors, checked all the windows, and turned out the lights; he even remembered to check his answering machine. Then, having worked himself into a state of incandescent lust, he went upstairs as quickly as he could manage.

He went up the stairs and past the stained-glass window without a second thought. A soft light shone from beneath the bedroom door; he heard Penny's voice, deep and breathy and familiar, calling out, inviting him in. He even imagined that he heard faint sounds of movement as she climbed onto that feather mattress, arraying herself for his view. He was expecting nothing but an uproariously good tumble.

Penny's voice was seductive and teasing. "Ringan? Come along; private view, just for you."

Smiling, breathing quickly, he laid a hand on the door.

It hit him like a hammer, a wave of intense cold, much worse than it had been before. Breath and voice alike froze in his chest, and stuck there. The dark hallway suddenly seemed full of an invisible mist, whose particles were clammy ice. A tiny whimper painfully forced its way through his constricted throat.

"Ringan!" The voice was high, torn. In his state of consummate fear, it took him a moment to put a name to it. *"Ringan!"*

Penny. She was in there, and whatever it was, was in there with her.

His knees were rubbery and useless; only his hands on the door held him upright. He couldn't move. But he had to move. Penny was in there. And something was wrong.

He tightened his hands around the knob, and pushed. The latch clicked, and the door swung open. The air felt as dense and as heavy as quicksand. He propelled himself into the bedroom and clung to the door, fighting vertigo and trying to focus.

Penny was on the bed, pressed up against the headboard. She was wearing what seemed to be a few lacy strings, and nothing else. If he'd been woried that she would yearn toward this ghostly intrusion, as she had seemed to yearn toward the earlier encounters in the barn, his worry was groundless. Her pose was a peculiar mixture of terror and belligerence; one fist was pushed up against her mouth, but the other was clenched, and ready to launch a good solid haymaker at the first jaw that presented itself.

Ringan noticed, with complete irrelevance, that something had happened to the antique quilt; it had changed colour somehow, and texture too, going from a hand-patched blue gently faded by the passage of time to strong lines of shade, and the brilliance of rough dyes. The room reeked of lavender, mixed with something musty and rotting.

Penny was not alone on the bed.

The revenant was there, or partly there. Even in his weakness and terrified nausea, he was astounded. Betsy, if this had in fact once been a girl named Betsy, was beautiful beyond belief. She was a mutable figure, flickering from what looked like anthropomorphic smoke to something nearly solid. In either state, she was staggering. Black curls fell in a cloud to a tiny waist, and huge eyes the color of storm clouds sat in a piquant, finely boned face. Her hands were small and rough; they curled into the stuff of the coverlet that had not been there before Penny and Ringan had entered the room.

Her dress was difficult to see clearly. Still, Ringan noted hazily that Penny had been right; it was of the Napoleonic era. If Betsy had been flesh and bone, she would have stopped traffic from London to Glasgow. She was drop-dead gorgeous. In fact, perhaps because of her colouring, she bore an unnerving resemblance to Penny.

As if she had suddenly become aware of him, she turned the enormous gray eyes in his direction, opening her mouth, making as if to speak. Ringan wouldn't have thought it was possible to grow any colder, but that gesture, the very reality of her taking notice of him, did it. One hand lifted, as if in greeting, and then went to the base of her neck, where it met the shoulder. The gesture was slow, graceful, redolent of a pain beyond words. Ringan made a noise in his throat.

Penny moved. She went so fast that Ringan, already disoriented, saw only a blur as she came out of her tight fetal curl, launching herself off the bed and across the room. She got him painfully by the hair and wrenched him through the bedroom door. Her body, most of which was visible between the interstices of her frivolous teddy, was shaking. Her face was the colour of old putty.

She kicked the bedroom door shut behind her, closing in the lovely, unnatural creature, the smell of death and lavender. Transferring her grip from Ringan's hair to his arm, she pulled him into the smaller bedroom across the hall.

Then, as unexpectedly as it had begun, the ordeal was over. The air warmed and lightened, the flowery scent faded. Ringan, who had slid to the braided rug and ducked his head between his knees, felt the crippling nausea ease. His strength returned, as quickly and thoroughly as it had been sapped. In seconds, Lumbe's was clear. The air in the room was, once again, only the warm air of a June night.

"Bloody hell," Penny said thinly. "Bloody hell, bloody hell. Ringan?"

"It's fine, love. I'm fine. And you're fine, too." The paralysing vertigo receded, fading with the weakness and the scent of lavender. He was warming up again, too.

It was amazing how quickly he was coming back to normal. He wondered how much of that recovery speed was due to the fact that Penny, this time, had not been anything other than normal. That simple fact was amazingly reassuring.

"What happened in there, Pen?"

Penny, badly shaken, told him her story. She'd gone upstairs and got undressed, rummaged in her grip until she'd found the bit of rude underwear she'd brought along, and struggled into it. Which, she pointed out, was no mean feat, considering it laced in the back . . .

"Believe me, I noticed," Ringan told her. "Go on."

There was little more to tell. She'd heard him on the stairs, climbed onto the bed, and called for him to come in. Almost at once, two things happened simultaneously; the air around her seemed to fill up with the smell of lavender, and someone— something—materialised at the foot of the bed.

"I know this sounds absurd, but I swear it's true. My first reaction was outrage." She shook her head in disbelief, a pale figure in a room full of starlight. "I didn't make the connection. Isn't that insane? Lavender, and a shadowy lady dropping in from the sixth dimension or somewhere, and my first thought was, who's this tart and how dare Ringan think I'd be into a threesome? No connection. E. M. Forster would be ashamed of me. I'm ashamed of myself."

Ringan pulled himself off the floor. " 'Only connect'? I know. At what point did you connect, if you don't mind my asking?"

"When I realised that my skin was crawling, that I'd gone ice-cold, that my legs felt like strands of overcooked pasta, and oh, by the way, when I got a look at her dress." Penny was still shaken. "I can't believe how long it took me to understand. I suppose the human mind doesn't take readily to accepting ghosts."

"Neither does the human body," he pointed out wryly. "I am as limp as a noodle, or at least my legs are. Still all weak and trembly. What a waste."

"Waste?"

"Well," he said, considering her, "if you could only see what you look like in that naughty little bit of nonsense you're wearing, you'd understand that limpness is not an appropriate reaction."

"How nice of you to say so." She considered him from the dimness, her gleaming eyes at variance with her mouth, which was under imperfect control. "So, do we dare go back into Bluebeard's chamber? Or not?"

"We dare," he said strongly. "This is my house, Penny. I've earned Lumbe's Cottage and I've earned that barn. I worked for it, it's my home, and that happens to be my bedroom across the hall. I am not going to be shut out of my own bedroom by a succulent succubus. If she shows up again, I'll threaten her with an exorcist or find some holy water or something."

"Get off it," Penny said, sounding more like herself. "Holy water? Exorcist? And you a good Protestant."

"Well, maybe garlic would work, or crosses, or a good sharp stake. Or are those just for vampires?" He put an arm around her.

"Seriously, Penny, I meant what I said about going back in. I don't have a choice. After all, I'm going to have to come to grips with this mess eventually, aren't I? I live here now. I can't spend forever ducking it. It seems to me that once we find out who she is—well, was—we can find out how she died. And when we do that, we'll be halfway to reclaiming the house."

"Will we?"

"I think so. If all the ghost stories are accurate, we ought to be able to find out why she walks the halls and stairs of Lumbe's, and how to put her back to sleep." The idea had settled into the forefront of his mind, and wanted to be looked at properly. Exorcism? Was it even an option? As Penny had pointed out, Ringan came from a long line of Scots Protestants; all he knew about exorcism was some actress's head spinning around, and a priest being involved. He pushed the image away. "Still, that's for tomorrow. Right now, madame, I cordially invite you to show me the strings on that bit of froth you're wearing in a better light. In fact, I insist."

"Mmm. Right." She stood still, her eyes half-closed, as he rubbed one hand along her hip. "Does this mean you've stopped being limp as a noodle?"

"You're damned right it does," he said, and reached for the laces of the teddy.

Jane Castle drove from Plymouth to Glastonbury, and got into town at two o'clock.

She didn't call Lumbe's straight off. Like many small people with high metabolism, she had an enormous appetite; driving was only one of many things that made her hungry. She parked the car, grabbed the hard-shell case that held her flute—the instrument was sterling silver, eighty years old, and she was not about to leave it in the boot of her Vauxhall—and headed up the High Street in search of sustenance.

When she emerged from a small café, it was past three o'clock, and she was replete with the effects of a well-cooked, hearty meal.

Idly, she mulled over her available options. She could call Ringan, or have a nice wander through Glastonbury, or hunt up a luthier's shop Liam had told her about, which was supposedly superb. What she really wanted was a shot of the local West Country cider, but on that score she was out of luck; the pubs wouldn't open till six. Ah well, she hoped, Ringan had shown enough sense to lay in a stock of cider; knowing Ringan, it seemed likely.

She went down the hilly street and found a phone kiosk. Ringan's answering machine greeted her. He'd left a recorded message with detailed directions to Lumbe's. Jane, who was not very good with directions, had to turn her purse inside out hunting for a pencil, and eventually called the machine three times before she'd gotten it all down.

That taken care of, she tucked the scribbled map into her pocket and decided to have a stroll around Glastonbury before braving the unfamiliar country lanes. The weather was lovely; bright, sunny, and warm.

She fetched up at the luthier's shop after all, having ducked down a side street in search of a bookshop and discovered a window full of handmade instruments quite by accident. After a blissful hour, during which she exchanged envious noises and compliments with the proprietor (an amateur flutist who professed to worship the ground Jane walked on), she tore herself away and went back to the Vauxhall. It was high time, she thought, that she made her way to Lumbe's Cottage.

After a wrong turn had somehow left her on a road barely wider than her car, circling round Glastonbury Tor for what seemed like hours, she managed to right herself. Lumbe's proved easy to find after all, since Ringan's Alfa was parked out front of the cottage, in full view of the road.

But he wasn't home. Repeated knocking on the front door produced no response. Exasperated, Jane rattled the doorknob and found it locked. Further exploration revealed the door to the kitchen. That was locked, as well.

Well, thought Jane irritably, this was just lovely. Invite a guest, leave instructions for getting there, and then scarper before the guest arrives. Obviously, Ringan and Penny had gone out, either for a long walk or, more likely, in Penny's car. Either way, Jane was damned if she would spend the next who knew how long huddled in her own vehicle. And she certainly wasn't going to drive anywhere else; the encounter with Glastonbury Tor had been quite enough for one afternoon. Oh, well, at least the weather was pleasant.

Very pleasant, in fact. The air was delightfully warm, the sun dappled the cottage walls, and birds and insects flavored the breeze with their voices. There was also a nice earthy smell, presumably coming from the charming herb garden planted hard by the kitchen door. Jane, somewhat drowsy, let the smells and sounds and general warmth play on her senses. After a bit, she settled down on the dry grass and leaned her back against the bottom half of the kitchen door.

Even through half-opened eyes, her surroundings were charming. There was a dancing stream, which seemed to be making an ungodly racket for so small a body of water. On its far bank, there was an orchard of apple trees; on this side of the stream, a small old building that looked like a scaled-down barn with a genuine thatched roof. The sun touched her hands, and she let them relax into the warm grass. Nice, Jane thought, and realised how fuzzy and comfortable she felt. Very nice indeed. A perfect setting for a little nap . . .

When she came back to full wakefulness, she was confused and logy. My God, she wondered, how long was I dozing? She glanced at her watch, and was surprised that only fifteen minutes had passed. She stood up, trying to shake the pins and needles out of her legs, and looked around the corner of the house. There was still no sign of Penny's car. Wobbling a bit, Jane walked to the edge of the road and peered in both directions. The only thing visible for miles was a slow-moving tractor, toy-sized in the distance.

There was no point in standing about like a tacky lawn sculpture. Hoping that her hosts would get themselves back home before her need for a loo became urgent, Jane decided to make the best of the wait. She set off to explore the boundaries of Ringan's new property.

She went first to the stream. It was odd, she thought, that its voice was so loud; it was even odder that, through some bizarre trick of natural acoustics, she was able to hear it, no matter her distance from it. She was so fascinated by this phenomenon that she deliberately walked back to the cottage, closed her eyes, and stood listening. There was no mistake; the sound of moving water remained at a steady, even volume, the same here as it was at the stream's edge.

Jane puzzled over it, walking slowly away from Lumbe's and glancing around. If there had been hills or trees to impact the acoustics, it might have been understandable, but the only trees in any quantity were across the stream, and couldn't possibly affect things. As it was, the thing was a mystery. She wondered if Ringan had noticed it.

She was so deep in thought that she nearly walked into the side of the barn before she caught herself. Startled, she put out a hand and leaned against the building. As her fingertips connected with the stone and wood, she suddenly went very still. She cocked her head to one side, wondering if her ears were playing tricks on her.

No, they weren't. Someone nearby was humming a tune.

Jane Castle was a consummate musician. Unlike Penny, she had no difficulty putting a name to the song; she recognised it at once. True, the melody was slightly different from the one currently in use among Jane's fellow musicians, and there was something odd about the singer's voice; it was a deep baritone, very masculine, tuneful enough, but it seemed to be fading in and out, as if the singer was at a great distance. But he wasn't, and Jane knew it. Whoever was humming, with pain and loss and regret in the very timbre of his voice, was on the other side of the wall. He was in the barn.

As she listened, wondering and intent, the humming faltered and changed into song. It became a lyric, a light smattering of words. The words died, a melody once again.

Jane Castle respected music; it was her life. She loved music, and never gave a second thought to the impulses laid upon her by the deep and heady necessities of making music. She didn't stop to think now.

She hurried back to her car and retrieved her flute. There was a sense of urgency in her, a need to get back to the old barn, a feeling that she was somehow needed there. By the time she'd reached it again, the feeling of life and death urgency had taken a strong hold of her.

She circled the barn until she found the door. It was locked, the latch in place; the man must be locked inside. She touched the wood of the door, the metal latch itself. It was warm from the sun.

She opened her flute case and took the instrument in hand. What preparation was required took only seconds; she'd first picked up a flute on her sixth birthday, and could have either prepped or played in her sleep. Standing so that she faced that locked door, she listened to the invisible singer just long enough to identify the key in which he sang. Then, drawing breath, she raised the flute to her lips and began to play along.

The singing stopped, and so did Jane; it seemed as if the universe itself paused. There was a short silence, a peculiar breathy pause in time, as if the world had drawn into itself, and was waiting to see what would happen next. In an absolute quiet in which even the birds had stilled their voices, Jane heard the stream. It seemed louder now, pounding, roaring.

Holding the flute, she fixed her eyes on the door, opened her mouth, and sang. She knew the words to this particular song quite well. While it wasn't a standard in Broomfield Hill's regular rotation, they did cover it when the mood took them, every fourth or fifth show.

Her pure, chilly soprano cut across the afternoon like a surgeon's scalpel. It was the song that had come from the invisible singer behind those stone walls. *"I am a hand-weaver to my trade, I fell in love with a factory maid, and if I could but her favour win, I'd stand beside her and weave by steam . . ."*

With a tiny click, the latch on the barn door disengaged itself. Jane stepped back, and from five feet away watched it pop loose. The door swung open, as if in invitation.

Completely unafraid, and without a moment's hesitation, Jane walked into the barn.

Six

*How can you say it's a pleasant bed
When none lies there but a factory maid?
A factory lass although she be
Blessed is the man who would enjoy she.*

"Anything?"

Ringan, deep in the early part of the nineteenth century, jerked his attention back to the present and focussed on Penny. She sounded tired, and a bit frustrated.

"All kinds of things," he said cheerfully, "but nothing relevant to what we need. I've found the estate accounts for the summer of 1812. Interesting stuff, if you go for nice dry notations of cabbage harvests and sales of new lambs to the butchery in Street. Oddly enough, though, I find I actually do go for them." He cleared his throat. "Listen to this. '4 September, one calf, two pounds three shillings, sold to John Parker, Westhill Farm, Yatton.'"

"Fascinating," Penny said drily. "Simply too divinely interesting for words. Would you mind telling me what that has to do with—"

"If you'd let me finish, I would. Yatton's a good bit away from here; either the Wychsale family had a solid reputation in the county as cattle breeders, or else this bloke was an old customer, or a personal friend. I got sidetracked trying to find some mention of him elsewhere."

Penny's brows went up. "Well, did you?"

"Not yet." He was serious, she realised. Ringan had got caught, genuinely interested, in this prosaic scrap of everyday nonsense from two centuries past. *I should have expected it,* she thought;

after all, he's a historian and I'm not. He can sit here at the beginning of the twenty-first century, with sunlight coming through the windows of Albert Wychsale's lovingly restored muniment room, and honestly care about this Parker chap, whom he's never met, never even seen a picture of, and who's been dead forever. And even though he seems far more worried than I am about dealing with our ghosts, even though he stands to lose his house if he doesn't deal with them, he can turn that bit off and worry about someone called Parker. How in hell does he do it?

"Penny for them."

It took a moment, but she caught his meaning. "Oh, a penny for the Penny's thoughts? They wouldn't be worth it. I was only just mulling over the difference between us, I mean the difference in the way we each look at history."

"You mean that you enjoy the grand sweeping pageant of it all, the vast march of important events against the backdrop of great minds and passing centuries? And that I go chasing after trivial bits of mystery like John Parker of Westhill Farm, Yatton? True, very true."

"Well, not completely true." Penny felt an obscure need to defend herself; it was almost as if she were being indicted for having a superficial mind. "I like the smaller things when I can make some kind of, I don't know, connection to them. Or when they touch me, or pull some kind of chord in me somewhere. They have to be personalised, somehow. And in any case, I'm a theatre person. Grand sweeping pageants is rather what we do, isn't it?"

"I know what you mean." He sounded sympathetic, and she saw that he'd not only read her thoughts, but understood them perfectly. She was constantly being amazed at how quick and accurate his perceptions could be. "I found one of those connections myself, a few minutes ago. There's a listing in the 1812 household accounts register, a requisition for a dinner guest: three bottles of the best brandy and a young goose to be killed, to entertain the Reverend William Holland."

"Three bottles? Ah, obviously a pickled parson. So?"

"So, I was browsing about in one of the bookshops in Glastonbury, and came across a reprint, on the Local Interest shelves, and it was this Holland's diary. I read a few pages of the thing; he was a raging Tory, absolutely rabid when it came to Catholics and Methodists." He shot her a sidelong glance. "The thing is, when I found this entry in the household accounts just now, it rang a bell . . ."

"Almost as if you'd found mention of a friend? I see what you mean. But haven't you found anything at all about what we're looking for? Because frankly, darling, as nice as all these bits and bobs are, it's getting a wee bit tiresome. And we still have to go back to Lumbe's and sleep there tonight, and I'm damned if I want to head off next week and play Helen of Troy for the Danes if it means leaving you alone in the house with that gorgeous little tart we saw last night. My life is complicated enough as it is."

"What a realist you are." He was grinning. "Don't worry, I can safely say that she doesn't turn me on at all. Have you found anything about Lumbe's?"

"Only the name of the family that moved into it after it was rebuilt. Some people called Wall; that was in 1792. I've got up to 1800 on the dot, and they're still there, at least as far as I can tell. There's nothing to indicate that they've moved on, or anything. It's getting frustrating."

"A family called Wall." He got up, stretched, and came to peer over her shoulder. "I suppose that's a start. Could they be the people we're looking for?"

She shook her head. "I don't see how. The beamish boy in the barn was a weaver, I'd swear to that, and anyway he looked to be yeoman class. If these accounts are to be believed, the Walls were a labouring family. Poor as church rats and right at the bottom of the economic scale."

"But if they had a daughter?"

"That's the point, they didn't. The names are all here: parents, Peter and Sarah Wall, offspring in order of age, John, James, Michael, Thomas, and one infant that died of typhus during a bad local outbreak. All boys, the lot of them, including the dead infant. I think it's safe to say the Walls are out of the running for our particular needs."

"And besides, we're looking for the Napoleonic era," Ringan agreed. "Let's keep plugging away, shall we? We may have to call it a day soon. It would be really rude to have invited Jane and then leave her locked out-of-doors."

"True." Penny yawned cavernously. "What's the time, love?"

"Just gone three. Ah well, onward and upward."

For the next hour, the only sounds were the rustle of carefully turned pages and the occasional scrape of a pencil as Ringan made an entry in his notebook. Suddenly Penny gave an exclamation, and Ringan's head came up.

"Something?" he asked sharply.

"I think so. In fact, I hope so, because I'm getting a wretched case of eye strain." She rested her finger halfway down one densely written page. "A change in Lumbe's tenancy. 1802, and the Walls are gone; Papa, that would be Peter, appears to have died in some hideously gruesome accident involving a tun of apples and a cider press."

"Ugh, nasty. So?"

"So Mummy Sarah went off to finish her days at the work-house in Street, poor old thing, and a new family moved into Lumbe's. Name of Roper, and from the looks of it, your basic half-starved labourers—just what the doctor ordered. Damn this tiny little writing, I've misplaced it." She tilted her head and found the entry she wanted. "Here we are. Father was called George, apparently did jobs from harvesting to threshing to cleaning out stables. His wife's name was Anne. According to this, they have two children; a newborn called George, and a three-year-old girl named Elizabeth."

"Elizabeth?"

Penny stared at him. Ringan's eyes were glittering, and his mouth was taut with triumph. "What on earth?" she asked.

"Elizabeth," he said. "Well done, O love of my life. Excelsior, in fact."

"Really? Huzzah and hurrah, and how very clever of me. Would you mind telling me just why you think I've—" Her eyes suddenly widened. "Oh. Oh!"

"Sussed it out, did you?" Ringan took her hand, raised it to his lips, and planted a kiss on the inside of her wrist. "Elizabeth, my lovely. Betsy. Not so common a nickname as Eliza or Lizzie or even Bess, I'll grant you, but still—Betsy is a short form of Elizabeth."

They stared at each other, Ringan flushed with success, Penny wide-eyed and thinking hard. She spoke first.

"Ringan," she said, "you got a good look at her, didn't you? Last night, I mean."

"I certainly did. Why?"

"I've got a sort of idea; humour me. How old would you say she was?"

He closed his eyes and pushed his memory. What had he seen? Huge gray eyes, small yet sturdy bones, masses of dark hair, smooth unlined skin, a taut, muscular, compact body with a tiny little waist and generous bosom, small roughened hands that clutched as they faded in and out. "Hard to say," he said doubtfully. "Young, that's for sure. The problem is, they aged very quickly in those days. All that hard work, and they started early; it wore them out. At a guess, I'd put her age at seventeen, maybe eighteen. Certainly no older than that."

"That's what I thought," Penny agreed. "Well, that makes it easier, doesn't it? Narrows things down?"

Ringan blinked at her. "Does it? How?"

She tapped the massive register she'd been reading. "You're not thinking," she told him. "The Ropers moved into Lumbe's in 1802, and the little girl Elizabeth is mentioned as being three years old. If we had to, we could check it in the parish records; I'm sure there's a big fat juicy register of births and deaths for you to find connections in. So she was born in 1799. Say she was seventeen at the time of her death . . ."

Ringan finished the math aloud. ". . . that would put us at 1816. That was the year after they fought Waterloo. Napoleonic period dress indeed, Pen. What good eyes you've got."

"So what on earth are we waiting for?" Penny's eyes were ablaze with interest; her need for a personal connection had been met. Betsy, the unnatural, cold-inducing flicker of abnormal light that had invaded Ringan's bed had just become Elizabeth, the hard-working daughter of a family called Roper, with a father named George and a mother called Anne. To Penny, the ghost was now a girl. "Where's the register for 1816? Give it here."

"Wait, I'm looking." Ringan's careful hands, mindful of the value and fragility of the huge registers, contrasted strangely with his eager voice. "Oh, bloody hell!"

"What is it?" Penny came and stood beside him. "What's the matter?"

"It's not here, that's what's the matter! I've got the pile from 1790 up through 1815, and that's where it stops. Damn, damn, damn!" He got to his feet. "Where's that house phone? And what's the extension for Wychsale's librarian?"

"Seven." The voice, a pleasant reedy tenor, came from the doorway. "Dial one, wait, then dial seven."

Startled, they both looked up. The newcomer was a portly man in his forties, with an unexpectedly shy smile. He strolled in and nodded at them. "But don't bother, I'm right here. Good afternoon, Mr. Laine, Ms. Wintercraft-Hawkes. I just thought I'd pop along and see if you were finding everything all right, and apparently you're not. Lucky timing on my part. Is there something I can help you with?"

"Hullo, Dr. Wainfleet." Penny's social sense rarely deserted her; she gave John Wainfleet, the Wychsale House librarian and muniments master, her most endearing smile. They'd been introduced earlier that day by Albert Wychsale, and she'd already gone to some trouble to charm him. It was gratifying, she thought, to see that he'd responded as hoped; his chest puffed out and his eyes brightened as he looked at her. She gestured at the oak table, with its stacked volumes and scattered notes, and said ruefully, "I'm afraid we've run into a roadblock. The registers only go through 1815, and we need a year or two past that. Could you help?"

"I wish I could, and normally, there would be no problem. But not today, I'm sorry to say." The librarian sounded genuinely regretful. "The volumes for 1816, 1817, and 1822 aren't here at the moment. One of the maids left a window open in here, and those three were out at the time, and they got a bit damaged round the edges. They've been sent off to Cardiff for rebinding. And I'm afraid they're not due to be returned here until this Wednesday at the earliest."

The man in the barn had stopped singing.

Jane Castle was an emotional woman, but she was no fool, and she was deeply sensitive. She trusted her senses, and her intuition; she had good reason to. For a long time to come, she would wonder why those senses had taken so long to inform her that something out of the ordinary was taking place in the barn.

At the time, they offered no warning. One foot moved, and then the other, carrying her across the threshold.

The first thing she noticed was the sound of running water. She'd been hearing the stream all along, but now it was louder than ever. The steady, unvarying pulse had puzzled her out-of-doors. Now, surrounded by the old stone walls, it had become a deep heavy Niagara, an invisible freshet that rang in a rhythmic pounding from the highest reaches of the crucked roof. It was almost as if the barn itself had a panic-stricken heartbeat. Yet, oddly, the building had no touch of damp. It was cool, with a clean dry smell to it.

"Where are you?" she called out, and her voice caught and spiralled against the sound of the water she could not see. "Hello? Why are you hiding? It's all right, you can come out."

She felt no fear, no unease, only a deep desire to help. And that was interesting too, that she should feel so strongly that the singing man was hurt, wounded in spirit if nowhere else, somehow in need of her comfort and aid. So evocative had that pleasant, distant voice been of pain and loss that Jane's palms itched with the need to help him.

But between the opening of the barn door and her first step inside, he had vanished. And that was impossible. The windows were shuttered and bolted, there was no second door. Unless he'd turned to smoke and drifted through some tiny crack between all that plaster and wood and cob there was simply nowhere else he could have gone. He had to be in here somewhere.

"Hell," she muttered. "Come on, chap, where are you?"

There was no response, but for a moment the beat of the stream seemed to grow even louder. It was unpleasant, that noise; it was oddly alive, a pulse where none should be. It made her skin crawl, touched her with the sense that she was smaller than she knew herself to be.

Jane decided to drown it out with a noise of her own. She raised her flute, fitted her lips to the mouthpiece, and trilled a few bars of the song he'd been singing.

She knew he was there, behind her, before those first notes died on the still air. His presence was unheralded by sound, but she knew he was there, all right. She'd never been so aware of anyone in her life.

She lowered the flute and turned quickly. If the sudden jerky motion startled the man, he didn't show it. He stood quietly, looking at her, staring into her eyes while seeming to look straight through her.

Her first thought, that he was in need of some gentle but firm fashion advice, came and went in a hurry. Her second thought was the realisation that her senses had betrayed her. There was no man here; this was illusion, only a semblance of life, and not the thing itself.

The man was not solid, not corporeal, not real at all. She could clearly see the outline of a pile of straw behind him, on the floor against the wall. She could have put a hand straight through him and met no resistance.

Her third thought, clearest by far, was that the rushing water had not only got into the barn, but into her bones as well. She was cold, she was freezing, she was soaked through, every hair and every pore was permeated with stream water. Her blood was forming minute icy crystals, processing that water by some oblique human chemistry, and it was because of him, this man, this—this revenant.

That's it. God in heaven, that's what it is. He's a revenant, a ghost.
This is absolutely incredible. I'm sitting here staring at a dead bloke, and
the dead bloke's staring right back at me. So why aren't I terrified half out
of my wits?

It was true, she wasn't at all frightened. Cold, yes, she was chilled
to the bone, but it wasn't the cold of fear; he'd just brought some
smell of his own mortality along with him, and she was picking it
up, some rarely used instinct acting like antennae on an insect, or a
snake's tongue, scenting the air, identifying what was safe and what
was not. Some of it was the water, too. Anyway, the cold was easing
up.

It occurred to Jane suddenly, even as it had occurred to Ringan,
that the situation was ludicrous. She was face to face with a ghost,
a revenant, something was dead and alive at the same time and she
ought to be scared blind; that was the conventional reaction to
encounters with the invisible world, wasn't it? All the books said so.

She wasn't scared at all. She still wanted to help him, and nothing more.

She stared at him openly, frankly studying him. It was a bit difficult, since he kept wavering in and out; it was rather like trying to
map out the details of a face as seen through rain-streaked glass.
But she needed to see him, and she kept her vision on him, absorbing him. Something in fifteen generations of Castle women,
women who were singers and healers and midwives and in some
instances had burned for their skills and their sensitivity, had sharp-
ened itself to deal with this very moment in Jane's life. She had to
see him. She had to help him. She had to know.

He had—or had had, once upon a time—a very nice face, open
and good-tempered. There were lines of care around his eyes, but
there were also lines of laughter, and the eyes themselves were
brown and alert. His hair was dark, curling profusely from a wide
brow and strongly delineated temples. His cheekbones were broad,
and his lips full; his nose, which looked as though it had been on
the losing end of too many childhood battles, was crooked and
bumpy. He was powerfully built, though compact in height. And
he had nice hands, excellent hands in fact, sensitive and long-

fingered, the hands of an artisan or a musician. Those hands weren't empty, either. One hand held what looked like some sort of tool. A closer look, and Jane changed her mind; it was not a tool but a toy, a carved wooden model of something Jane couldn't identify.

He moved, the barest twitch of his head and shoulders.

"It's all right," Jane said quickly, softly. Her voice, at its clearest, was soothing and insistent, a gentle persuasive belltone. "Really, you don't need to be afraid. I won't hurt you. I—I'd like to help you. Will you let me do that?"

He turned his head to stare at the pile of straw behind him. It was a simple gesture, made without theatrics, but it took Jane like a fist in the pit of the stomach. Longing came from him in waves, an impression of loss and need that was unbearably poignant. Tears rose to her eyes, and her fingers closed hard around her flute.

"Don't," she said gently. "Please don't suffer so much, I can't bear it. Let me help you—let me try. Please?"

If he heard her, he made no sign. He kept his eyes fixed on the empty pile of straw. Jane, helplessly caught in the backwash of long-dead feelings that, while not her own feelings, were nonetheless too strong to fight, turned her gaze to follow his, and made a discovery.

The straw bed—it was interesting, that she should know what it had been used for—was not solid either. The barn's beaten floor was visible beneath it. It was a part of his world, his life, and not hers.

And something was happening on that misty pile, something was coming, making itself from nothing more than dancing motes of dust and the deep memories this place seemed to hold. Jane saw patches and lines, colours both dull and bright, and finally understood their significance: this was a piece of hand-weaving, a picture of a girl woven into cloth. A girl with black hair that fell to her slender waist, in a drab-coloured dress. A girl who stood with one arm stretched out beneath an apple tree, hard by a very familiar, if simply rendered, cottage. Jane saw a puffy woven cloud, a little stone bridge in interlocking yarns.

The cloth flickered, died away into nothing, and the girl's features with it. Grief poured from the boy, a sorrow that bit like whip strokes.

"Who are you?" Jane asked. The urgent, insistent edge to her own voice startled her. She couldn't remember the last time something had disturbed her to such a degree.

Yet she wanted his attention, all of it. She wanted this poor doomed boy to acknowledge her, communicate with her, let her into the secrets of whatever cataclysm had brought him down, ending his life, leaving him stranded in some hellish replay of the thing that had destroyed him. "Talk to me," she said sharply, and her voice spiralled high and strident. "Damn it, who are you? Who were you?"

He moved then, away from Jane and toward the straw bed. She stepped forward without thinking, acting purely on those newly-honed instincts, matching his motions, until the dead man and the living woman stood before the pile of straw. They were no more than a foot apart.

He dropped to a knee. One hand, the empty one, he laid on the straw, denuded now of its bright coverlet, its black-haired girl, its apple tree. He extended the other, offering the carved wooden toy as if at an altar of worship. It came to rest in the precise center of the bed.

It's for his lover. This was their bed, and something happened here, something terrible, and he died. Maybe they both died. No wonder I want to help him. All the world loves a lover, doesn't it? All the world loves a . . .

"Betsy," said the revenant, and he was looking straight into Jane's face from centuries away. His voice was as mobile as birdsong, as high and as low as the wind in the apple trees, as unstoppable as the stream itself, moving inexorably toward the sea.

Jane's heart was slamming against her chest, she was burning hot, she was cold too. She seemed to be travelling a long way, all the way down into the secrets in those long-buried brown eyes and out the other side.

"Wait," she whispered, not knowing what she did, and reached out blindly with the hand that clutched her precious flute. From a great distance, she saw his eyes widen and his mouth open. It was as if, after all these years waiting in whatever nameless bit of ether he inhabited, something finally had the capacity to surprise him.

He reached out and touched the flute.

For the eternity it took for the shockwave to travel the length of Jane's arm to her heart and mind, she stood and gaped. Where the instrument and the young man came together, Jane saw a light-storm, a pulsing burning shower of the coldest rainbow possible. She knew him. She knew his passions, his patience, his life, and his losses. She knew his name, as well. And she knew his flesh, as the silver flute merged with the travesty that was an unnatural parody of living flesh, running together, expanding and exploding in silence.

"Gone," said the ghost, and then he was.

Jane Castle collapsed in a shaking puddle. Her eyes had rolled back in her head, her breathing was shallow and rapid, her senses completely overloaded. The shock of contact had brought something with it; in the seconds before the young man faded, she had seen his life, his love, and his death.

"Is it my imagination, or do I smell rain?"

"Not your imagination. I smell it too." Penny, not taking her eyes from the road, sounded relaxed. "Isn't that weird? It must be the last original natural instinct we've got, being able to smell changes in the weather. Lord knows, as a species, we've forgotten damned near everything else. And there's definitely rain on the way. Goodness, aren't we mystical?"

"Not really, it's just that my knee is acting up. It always does when a weather front comes through. Sorry to shatter illusions about the descendant of the Picts, listening for pounding hooves with one ear to the ground." Ringan stared out the Jaguar's window, at a virginally cloudless sky. "So we get to wait until Wednesday. Damn."

"Frustrating, isn't it?" Penny agreed. "Just when we'd reached a starting point. But we don't really have to wait for the Wychsale registers to get back, do we? Can't we find the information some-where else?"

"We could, if we knew what we were looking for," Ringan said gloomily. "Ah, sod it. If we're stuck, we're stuck; I'll just keep my eyes open and get ready to sleep in the Jag if the house gets too haunted for comfort. What do you want to do about dinner tonight?"

"Eat some. Actually, I'm starved. Those dainty little sandwiches Wychsale sent in barely took the edge off, you know? Watercress and chopped egg on bits of white fluff with the crusts gone simply aren't enough. I wonder what it is about that kind of desk work that's so hunger-making." Penny slowed down, swerved sharply around a pothole, pronounced a nice traditional Elizabethan epi-thet, and straightened the car. They rounded the last hedgerow before the turn into Lumbe's. "We ought to take Jane out and buy her a pint anyway, assuming she got here."

"She did. There's her car." Ringan was conscious of a twinge of guilt. After all, he'd told Jane to come along. Heaven only knew how long she'd been waiting. "I hope she's not too annoyed. Give me a moment, I need to gird my loins and prepare for a lecture on my rotten manners. I deserve one."

"Oh, well, at least we got home before the weather changed. Leaving her out in a Somerset rainstorm, now that would really be bad manners." Penny eased the Jag into the drive and killed the engine. "Look, she's gone off to explore. Her car's empty."

"And she's left the top down. We'd better find her before it starts to pour."

Penny locked the car and followed Ringan across the grass. She stopped abruptly.

"Ringan! Listen."

"I hear it." His ears had caught the high, muffled piping. There was something about the sound that raised the hair on his arms; what might not have rated a second thought in London, in this rural setting, seemed uncomfortably like the distant echo of pan-pipes. He changed direction, and headed for the barn.

"That's Jane," he said. "That's her flute. What in hell . . . ? Penny, what is it? What are you staring at?"

"It's the song." Penny's face had tightened into a kind of concentrated intensity. "The song, the one I heard, that you couldn't hear. She's playing it. God, how beautiful."

Ringan stopped in his tracks, and swivelled round to face her. "This song? This is what you heard?"

"I said so, didn't I?" Her muscles relaxed, leaving her face soft. She swallowed hard; when she spoke again, her voice was soft too. The melody washed across the grass, and as if the invisible flutist were some incarnation of the Pied Piper, Penny took an involuntary step toward it. "Oh, how lovely, how gorgeous. It makes me want to curl up and cry, or put my arms around you, or—or something, I don't know what. It gets me, it hits me somewhere, I don't even know where or why, but it does. Too much beauty. Honestly, too much."

"Do you know, dear," he said dryly, "I wish to high heaven that you were not quite so musically constipated. If you'd been able to hum even three bars of this damned thing for me when you first heard it, you'd have saved us some trouble."

He turned and headed for the barn. Penny, her head straining toward the music like a plant to the sun, hurried after him. "Ringan," she called, "wait a bit. Did you leave the barn door open? Unlatched?"

Ringan halted in his tracks. "No I didn't, now you mention it. In fact, I locked it and tested the lock."

They looked at each other, both faces reflecting a growing worry. The flute abruptly stopped.

"Christ," Ringan said, and ran.

The barn door was hanging wide, the interior showing as a dark, shadowed patch. Ringan swore under his breath, and shouted. "Jane! *Jane!*"

There was no reply. He laid a hand on the old wood, gathered his courage, and walked inside.

She was sitting on the floor, leaning her back against the wall. She cradled her flute in her arms like a child.

"Jane?" Penny had come up behind him. "Ringan, is she here? Did you find her? Oh—Jane!"

"Hullo, Penny. Hullo, Ringan." Jane raised her head and tried to bring them into focus. Her voice was dreamy. Even in the dimness, they could see that her eyes were all iris, the pupils virtually nonexistent. Surely that was wrong? In this dim light, her pupils should have been enormous, trying to adjust, and yet her eyes were all nacreous pools of gleaming colour. Ringan thought that she looked as if she'd smoked about a kilogram of hashish, and remembered abruptly that Penny's eyes had performed that same unnatural trick of trying to focus light with no pupils. "How nice that you finally got home," she said happily. "Did you know you've got a ghost in your barn?"

"There's another one, up at the cottage." Penny heard her own words, shook her head in disbelief, and pulled herself together. This won't do at all, she thought firmly. There was a peculiar atmosphere in the barn, something decidedly surreal. "Come on, Jane, up you get. Let's get out of here before it starts raining. You need to put the top of your car up. Don't want the upholstery all flooded, do you?"

"That's not rain." Jane sounded drunk. "That's just the stream. Awfully loud, that stream is. I'm not surprised, all things considered. I'm not surprised at all."

Penny and Ringan exchanged a wordless look over her head. By tacit accord, Ringan took one of Jane's arms, and Penny got a firm grip on the other. "Come on," Ringan told her. "Up you get. Time to head out of here."

"Up?" Jane said wonderingly, as though the word were one she'd never heard before and wanted to explore. Then she shrugged. "Up. Right. Here I come."

She followed them out of the barn on legs as unsteady as a newborn colt's. The outside air affected her immediately; she blinked violently, shook herself, and sucked in air. Her pupils widened, contracted, widened again.

"Goodness." Her voice was slurred. "My goodness. I feel—I don't know what I feel. Penny? Ringan?"

"It's all right, love." Penny slipped one hand under Jane's elbow and nodded to Ringan. "Lock that damned door, will you? We don't need any more adventures in the barn tonight; I'd say we've done our share for the day. She's all right, she's coming back. Jane? Jane love, are you better now?"

"Yes." She sounded more like herself. "Bloody hell. I just had the most—the strangest—you won't believe what happened in there."

"Oh, I expect we will." Ringan shot the bolt home. "Jane, can you tell us what happened?"

"Not now." Penny glanced up at the sky, which in the past few minutes had lost its hard bright edge. Clouds hurried across the horizon; above Glastonbury Tor, the air flashed molten with electricity. "Not here, not now. Let the poor girl get her breath back. It's going to come down in buckets in about five minutes, and we have to get the top of her car up. Let's do it, or we'll likely get washed out to sea."

They made the front door of Lumbe's just as the first long rumble of thunder rolled across the landscape. Jane, nearly back to normal, flinched; the air, supercharged with static, was not reacting well with her silver flute. She felt as if she were carrying a live wire.

"Quickly, everyone in." Ringan shoved Jane indoors, saw that Penny was already in the process of kicking off her shoes, and heaved a sigh of relief. He had no desire to be caught out of doors in a summer storm. The long, steady rain usual to the West Country was no problem, but an electrical outburst was as frightening as it was potentially dangerous. Even the slight contact between his fingertips and the old brass doorknob had given him a static shock. He decided to leave the chain off, and was glad of it a moment later, when a wild scratching at the door made him open it again. Butterball streaked between his ankles, his bright fur looking twice its normal density, mewing as he came.

"You poor baby." Penny, now barefoot, rubbed her fingers together in the classic gesture used to entice a cat. Butterball obliged by rubbing against her shins. Penny scratched behind his ears, and looked up to find Jane staring with her mouth open.

"That," Jane said weakly, "is an amazing animal. It's almost too beautiful. When did you get yourself a cat, Ringan? What's it called? And who's going to look after it when you're on the road with us, or off doing a house somewhere?"

"His name is Butterball, and not to worry, he's not mine. He belongs to my noble patron—or, if you believe my noble patron, the house, lands, and home farm belong to the cat. He just likes this cottage, that's all."

"So do I." Jane was nearly back to normal. She glanced around the room and said appreciatively, "If the upstairs is as nice as the downstairs, you're really in luck. If this were my place, the only way you'd get me out would be to carry me feet first. Screw down the coffin lid, laddies!" She watched Butterball jump into Penny's lap, purring contentedly and kneading. From the outside world came a crash of thunder; the shutters lit up with a brief glare as lightning silhouetted their outlines, and heated the air. "I'd say he likes the residents as well as the accommodations."

"Considering the amount of fresh cream we've been pouring down his throat, I'm not about to die of the shock," Ringan told her tartly. "Can we forget about that feline lump of adipose tissue for a moment? Jane, what happened out there?"

"I'll tell you, in a moment." She met his eyes. "But not just yet. First I want to hear about what's been going on here. I want to know if what I think I saw out there could possibly have been real. And I want to know why Penny said there's another ghost here, in the house."

"Because it's true." Penny, sitting cross-legged on the floor with her back against a chair leg, let her hand move rhythmically down Butterball's back. Her voice was nearly drowned out by the voice of the weather. It had begun to pour in earnest, a heavy noisy pounding of water against earth. "There is one—a girl. A very pretty girl, too."

"Betsy." Jane was nodding. "Betsy. She looks a bit like a young otherworldly you, Penny, assuming it's the same girl. Good grief, what am I saying, of course it's the same girl. Who else is it likely to be? Masses of superb black hair, gray eyes that take up half her face, a mouth like a Venetian courtesan?"

"That's her." Ringan was staring. "Are you saying you saw her out in the barn? Because if you did, you've seen something we haven't. We thought she was caught here, in the cottage. We've only seen the weaver boy out there—in fact, I haven't seen anything at all out there. Penny has, though."

"I saw her. But not really." Jane yawned suddenly, a wide, gaping yawn that made Ringan's jaws ache in sympathy. "Goodness, I'm feeling better. Tired, but better. I saw her through Will's eyes, on the weaving he made for her, and then later. I mean, the weaving he made of her. Well—both, actually. It was a picture of her, and a gift for her."

"Will?"

"William Corby. Your weaver lad. The boy with the generous mouth and the bumpy nose, not to mention the broken heart. The dead chap in the barn. His name was Will Corby."

Ringan's stomach had knotted up. He glanced over at Penny, and tried to convince himself that her expression—a rapt, concentrated, nearly unblinking gaze—wasn't disturbing. He failed miserably, and kept his voice very level. "How did you find out his name, Jane?"

"I didn't 'find out' anything," she said testily. "Will told me, or rather, he showed me. Ringan, you're being awfully dense today; it must be the weather. I was waiting for you to get home, and I decided to explore the grounds, and I heard someone singing." A minor grievance occurred to her. "And I must say, I think it's extremely rude of you, to tell me to come down and then give me wretchedly bad directions—I was half an hour circling round a cart-track at Glastonbury Tor—not to mention leaving me locked out in the wilds of Somerset. Why weren't you here to let me in? Where were you?"

"Up at Wychsale House," Ringan replied dryly, "poring over about eighteen thousand dusty vintage enormous tomes, that all seemed to be written with quills by people with a senseless passion for tiny, spidery letters. We were trying to find out the name of the weaver boy in the barn. Never mind that now, we're dying of curiosity. What happened out there?"

"I'm not sure I can tell it properly," Jane said slowly. "I mean, so much of it was bizarre, intuitive . . . it's hard to explain, really. I got here and you weren't home, so I went for a wander, and I noticed that no matter where I went, I could hear that stream out there. And the volume never changed, it was always just as loud no matter where I went. Why are you looking at me like that, Penny?"

"You too," Penny said quietly. "The first day I got here, I could even hear it in here." Her eyes were normal once more. "And I thought it had got into the barn, it was so loud in there. I knew it must mean something. Ringan couldn't hear it, could you, love?"

Ringan shook his head. "No. And I couldn't hear the music, either. Penny did, though."

"The music? You mean the singing? You really couldn't hear that? I can't imagine why not, Ringan, it was plain as day. In fact, it was the singing that took me over to that barn in the first place. I heard him singing, and of course I recognised the song. How could I not?"

"More than I did," Penny said gloomily, and Jane shot her a commiserating glance. She knew about Penny's problem with music. "Ringan's all cross with me because I couldn't hum it for him."

"I'm not cross, lamb, truly," he said gently, and Penny smiled across at him. "It's called 'The Weaver and the Factory Maid,' Penny. I'd have to say that ours is not the definitive version of it, but we do cover it occasionally, as a set freshener. Go on, Jane. Of course you recognised the tune. So did I, when I heard your flute."

"You'd have to be mental not to, wouldn't you? As you said, we do it every third or fourth show." Jane ran a finger down her flute. "Anyway, I was across the lawn but I knew it was coming from the barn. Don't ask me how, I just did."

"I know. So did I."

"Did you, Penny? Good on you. So, I went over to the barn, wanting to find the bloke and see if I could help. This is a bit tricky to explain . . ."

"No, I understand it," Penny broke in. "I had the same reaction, exactly the same. I was digging in the herb garden and I heard him and I just knew he was in some kind of awful muddle and he needed my help. I would have torn down the barn door to get in there."

"Just the same, then. Well, it was locked. So I stood outside and began singing with him, and I think I surprised him or something, because he shut up. I didn't want him to do that, so I played a bit of it, just a few bars. On my flute, I mean. And then the latch popped loose and the padlock fell off and the door swung open, and in I went."

She stopped abruptly, and they saw that she'd gone pale. Ringan turned and marched into the kitchen. He was back a few moments later, holding a tray with three glasses and a bottle of the local cider.

"You drink that," he ordered.

"Ringan, you must be telepathic." Jane accepted a glass and watched him pour two more. "I've been longing for some good West Country cider for absolutely hours. Cheers!"

"No telepathy was required, love. I know how much you like cider, that's all." He watched her take a long gulp from the brimming glass, waited for her to swallow, and prompted her gently, "Go on, now. What happened next?"

"I told you, I went in. And at first he wasn't there, I mean I couldn't see him." She looked across at Penny, who was watching her intently. "I think you'll follow this bit, Pen. I was wildly disappointed. And do you know, it didn't occur to me that anything odd was going on? Anything out of the ordinary, I mean. I heard someone singing inside a locked building, I watched the door unlock itself from the outside, I went in to find he'd vanished into thin air, and it all seemed normal." She took another mouthful of cider, and added thoughtfully, "That didn't last long."

"When did you realise . . . ?"

"When he popped up behind me. I couldn't miss it then, could I? Not if I'd been blind and mentally defective with it, I couldn't miss it. I went icy cold, and the stream sounded like Victoria Falls on a bender, and besides, I could see right through him. Now, *that* was a surprise."

Ringan grinned. "Ah. A dead giveaway, pardon the pun."

"Indeed it was. He was standing there in these ratty old clothes, all curly hair and broken nose, and I could see behind him to this pile of straw . . ."

"That's not real either. I saw it too." There was a concentrated, intent look in Penny's eyes. "Jane, did you see anything else? Other ghosts, other people, other pictures? Maybe of an even older time?"

Jane eyed her curiously. "No. No, I didn't. I saw Will—I knew his name after a bit, I'll get to that—and the straw bed, but I didn't see anything that didn't seem to have to do with him. That's what you mean, isn't it?"

"Yes. Damn. I hoped—no, never mind. Get on with your story, Jane. You knew he was a ghost, and then what?"

"We looked at each other, a real staring match. I kept trying to memorise his features, but it was tricky, because he kept washing in and out, as if I were seeing him through a gauze curtain that wouldn't stay still. And then I began to feel things—emotional things, memory things." She took a long pull at her cider. "That straw bed, for one."

"Grief, pain, tenderness. I know." Penny's mouth trembled. "Dear God, do I know. They used to meet there, I'm sure they did. Betsy and—Will, did you say?"

"Will Corby." Jane looked up curiously. "You really didn't get any of this, Ringan? Not hearing, or feeling it?"

"Not to this degree, no. I did get one minor bit of it, out in the barn. Penny says for a minute or two we weren't actually ourselves. She says my hands weren't my hands, that they were this Will bloke's. And I must admit, I had this huge surge of tenderness, a kind of need to shelter Penny, protect her from something. Now, that didn't feel normal at all. But of course," his mouth thinned to a line, "nothing about any of this feels normal to me. Have I mentioned I loathe it?"

"He usually lets me fend for myself," Penny told Jane confidingly. "He sees me as a bulwark and a shield, the ultimate pioneer woman, the stuff Empire was built on, mainstay of the colonies, making one little corner of his tithe barn forever England . . ."

"Shut up." Ringan grinned. "I let you fend for yourself because you'd take my head off if I didn't, and you know it. The thing is, Jane, it really didn't feel like me. I'm not much of a stroke, hug, and coo reassurances type generally, am I?"

"Ugh, no." Jane grimaced. "I'm surprised you weren't more sensitive to all the echoes around here, though."

"Oh, I'm sensitive enough. It's only that my particular receptors seem to pick up more on Betsy, that's all." His mouth thinned briefly into a taut line. "And I wish they didn't. My reactions aren't nearly so—so nurturing as yours are."

Jane raised her brows. "Nasty?"

"Let's just say that my primary response is not one of sympathy. This Betsy creature makes me break out in a kind of emotional rash. Maybe I'm allergic to ghosts."

"Maybe you are, but I don't seem to be. Anyway, I told you, I started seeing pictures, images. The straw bed first, and that woven cloth picture of Betsy he'd made—"

"Wait. Hang on a bit, can you? There's something . . ." There was a picture in Penny's memory, struggling for clarity. In the obedient silence that followed her request, she relaxed her mind. After a moment, it came clear. "You said, a woven cloth picture. It has a picture of Betsy on it. Yes?"

"Yes." Jane was staring. "Something?"

"Yes indeed, or at least, I think it's something. The thing is, I saw it in both places. It was on the bed, in contact with Betsy herself, the night she materialised in Ringan's room upstairs; she had a bit of it clutched in one hand. Ringan, you saw it there, didn't you? And we both saw it in the barn, I mean Jane and I did, on that bed of straw. And that makes it important somehow, because it's the only thing about all this that's shown up in both places."

"My God." Ringan tipped the rest of the cider down his throat and set his glass down hastily. "Penny, that's right, isn't it? You've heard the singing in both places, but you said it was distant and far-away when you heard it in the house. And you've heard the stream just as loudly here as you did in the barn, when you heard the singing in here. But an actual object?"

"This is the only thing." Penny's eyes were bright. "It's important, I know it is; it simply must be."

"A token," Jane said abruptly. "A love gift. Something he made for her, to give to her. And I think it's not the only token here. You know, I saw those images, things that were to do with Will. I saw them through Will's own eyes. And what started it was when he— Will, I mean—put this little wooden thing he was holding down on that heap of straw."

Penny flashed Ringan a smug look. "The handloom. The miniature handloom. A carved wooden thing, right?"

"Is that what it was? I wondered." Jane gave a long sigh. Taking this as an invitation, Butterball climbed off Penny's lap, stretched his front legs, and climbed into Jane's. She arranged herself to give him more room, dissuaded him from tenderising her trousers with his front claws, and closed her eyes. "And now I'm wondering if that was a token, too. Maybe a little something, from Betsy to Will?"

"This is getting very O. Henryesque, isn't it?" Penny spoke lightly, but her mouth was unsteady. "The whole 'Gift of the Magi' thing? I sold my hair to buy you the watch fob for your Christmas gift; you sold the watch to buy me the fancy combs for my lovely hair. My God, will you listen to that rain? What a lot of noisy water Somerset's got."

"That thing he was holding, I thought at first it might be for making music," Jane said dreamily. "But then I saw it was a toy of some kind."

"I think you've both nailed it. Tokens. It had to have been a gift, hadn't it?" Ringan, having emptied his glass, leaned back looking lazy and relaxed. "He'd hardly carry it about like that if it wasn't something special to him. Or given to him by someone special."

"And that would explain why the hold is so strong, so potent. A gift from Betsy. Even in death, he can't bring himself to put it down or abandon it." Penny stretched in much the same way Butterball had done. She looked like a cat herself, hedonistic, sensual, graceful. "Maybe that's what keeps him tied down here. We'll probably never know, because something that small isn't likely to have fetched up where we could find it, is it? No, I thought not. Ah well. A pity, but never mind. I suppose the cloth might be somewhere, mightn't it? In a private collection, or something. So he laid the thing down on the straw, and then what?"

"He spoke to me. Turned around, took the end of my flute in one hand, and spoke to me."

Ringan straightened up in a hurry. He shot a look at Penny, who was staring at Jane, slack-jawed. "He *spoke* to you?" Ringan asked incredulously. "Really to you, seeing you, I mean? Not just talking into the air?"

"He saw me, all right." Jane gave an involuntary shiver, and Butterball offered a soft protesting trill. "He took the end of the flute in his hand, and he looked right into my face, and he said one word. That's all. He said, 'Gone.' And the inside of my head exploded, and he faded out, and I watched him die."

There was a long silence, broken only by the insistent sounds of the weather. The storm was easing, its first wild outrage apparently spent. The thunder sounded more distant as it moved off toward Devon and Dorset, and the lightning now came intermittently. Penny's expressive mouth was working, and Ringan stared at Jane, chewing his lower lip.

"You know, this is bizarre." He was arranging his thoughts aloud; the purely intellectual side of the puzzle had, for the moment, overridden the emotional pull and ebb of the past two days. "Not just the ghosts, though I'll admit that being haunted is awfully damned peculiar. I mean our reactions to them. Is it only me, or do our reactions seem to be progressing with every encounter?"

"How would I know? I've only just got here." Jane pushed Butterball gently off her legs, and got up for more cider. "I haven't heard what's been going on with you two, not really, just in bits. I only know what happened to me, which is that I saw this one ghost very clearly, that he said something to me, that he took hold of my flute, and that when he did that I knew who he was, what his name had been. And when he did that, I saw a whole series of stuff they'd never put on the telly."

"Go back a bit, Jane, would you? Earlier on, you said you saw Betsy, and not just as a picture on a bit of woven cloth." Penny cocked her head to one side. "The storm's moving away, I think, or tapering off. When did you see Betsy, and how clearly? And how did Will Corby die?"

"He was murdered." Jane's hand shook; cider splashed over the edge of her glass and spattered on the floor. She kept her face averted, as if hoping that neither of her friends could see the white horror there. "Attacked and murdered. Whoever it was held him facedown in the stream until he drowned."

Ringan made a noise deep in his throat, a kind of whistling gurgle. Penny seemed to have stopped breathing.

Jane looked at her glass of cider as if she couldn't imagine where she'd gotten it, saw her own hands trembling, and carefully set the glass down. Her voice was flat and matter-of-fact.

"And whoever it was," she told her hosts, "they got Betsy too. She was stabbed, stabbed in the side of the neck, trying to pull the killer off Will, there in their bed, in the barn. That's how I saw Betsy—I saw her through Will Corby's eyes. That's what happened. I saw it happen."

Seven

A pleasant thought's come to me mind
As I turned down the sheets so fine
And saw her two breasts standing so
Like two white hills all covered with snow

"What I want to know," Penny asked drowsily, "is, does anyone have an idea? Anyone? Anything?"

"No." With an effort, Jane managed to tear her eyes from the bright warm heart of the fireplace; the embers, bursting into an occasional flare of temperamental flame, seemed to have partially hypnotised her. "Not about getting them out of here, anyway, if that's what you mean. Not about what to do. But I think the wind's dropping. Maybe the storm's blowing itself out completely."

"I suppose that would be something." Ringan sounded cranky enough to pose as the quintessential dour Scot. He was tired and drained, and beginning to feel resentful at having to worry about ghosts. Additional worry over the women was no help to his mood, either; first Penny, he thought, actually craning toward the dead people infesting the place as if she couldn't wait to find them and join the party, and now Jane, who seemed genetically incapable of the appropriate fear and loathing she surely ought to be feeling. What on earth was wrong with these women, anyway? "I don't know about you lot, but I'm knackered. I want my sleep. Me for some kip."

Penny, sprawled on the braided rug before the hearth, propped her chin on one hand and regarded him with sleepy affection. "An over-tired Ringan. Oh dear. Well, we can't have that, can we?" She suddenly gave vent to a cavernous yawn. "Our Ringan gets quite testy if he's sleep-deprived."

"I know, ducks. Quite unliveable, in fact. I've toured with him, remember?" Jane, sharing the rug with Penny and a curled-up Butterball, pulled herself upright and stretched her back. "I've been wracking my brains, but I'm coming up empty. Maybe we should try this again in the morning, after a few hours of beauty sleep." She considered this for a moment, then added fair-mindedly, "Of course, it's not all that far off morning now. Tell you what, I'll stay up and keep trying, if you will."

"No, I don't think so. If I don't get some rest, I'll be worse than useless, I'll be actively hostile." Ringan, with bedtime in sight, became more amiable. He reached out a hand and, with the ease of long practice, yanked Penny to her feet. "Come along, lamb. Young Ringan wants a wee nap. You're with me, so don't get any brilliant notions about a girl's chatfest in the guestroom. Shall we?"

"Yes, let's." Penny leaned against Ringan. "Jane, you've got the best spare bedroom, well, the only spare bedroom actually. Wait till you see it. It's a Sotheby's special, absolutely an antique auctioneer's delight."

"I can hardly wait. Lead the way, you two. Oh, wait. Should we do something about the fire, do you think? Or is it safe to leave it smouldering?"

"I don't see why not," Ringan said reasonably. "This was Lumbe's only heat source for, what, at least a hundred years. They would have used it for all their cooking, as well. The residents probably left it burning whenever they could afford fuel, and I don't think we're likely to burn the place down now." They started up the stairs, Ringan in the lead. The only light was a faint glow from the hearth. "You know, I've been wondering about Betsy Roper's family. We'd only got as far as the first records of their coming to Lumbe's. At that point, they only had one son, and Betsy. Which is strange."

"Why?" Jane asked the back of Penny's neck.

"Because the labouring classes generally ran to biggish families," Penny answered for Ringan. "They had to, since maybe one out of three babies would survive infancy. I've wondered about that, as well. I suppose it's possible they lost a few babies along the way; we've no clue how old the parents were, after all. There was another reason for unbridled fecundity back then. The more babies a working-class family could produce, the more people in the family could go out and earn wages. Remember, children of five were sweating out in the manor's fields, ten hours a day, six days a week."

"But that's horrible!"

"No child labour laws," Ringan said briefly. He had cleared the landing and reached the upper level; they could hear him fumbling around for the light switch. "You know, it's taking me too long to learn my way about the place."

The sound from downstairs should have alerted them. Butterball, alone and unseen in his place of comfort before the fireplace, had lifted his head. His golden fur, so soft and dense, became spiked with alarm; his pupils contracted to black slits. He let out a long low snarl, a deep sound that rose and thinned and swelled to the rafters, becoming the unearthly cry of a cat who knows that something off, something that is a wrong thing, has come too close.

Penny stopped on the landing, so abruptly that Jane nearly trod on her heels and fell back two steps. Penny was a long dark patch against the oval window. She stood, breathing deeply and evenly, and as she stood, the wind outside shredded a passing cloud and a thin shaft of moonlight lit her like statuary in a cathedral niche. She blinked, and lifted a hand to her brow. "Betsy? Come out, lady. Are you here?"

"Don't!" Jane had frozen in place, as a rabbit freezes when it scents the fox. Something had happened to Penny's voice. It was pitched high, too high, thin and slurred at the same time. Her accent had changed subtly. And something was wrong, there was something in the air, it was icy, it was freezing . . .

"Ringan!" Jane cried out, in primal terror. *"Ringan!"*

"What in hell . . . ?" Ringan found the switch and flipped it on, and the upper floor was bathed in soft light. He turned to look behind him, as the first touch of the hated and familiar lassitude took his knees, his spine, and turned them to chilly powder. Six feet behind him, the landing was a well of deep shadow. "What . . ." His voice was a thin thread, barely a whisper. "No . . . I can't . . ."

Invisible in the black turn of the lower stairway, Jane was an ice woman. In her mind, she was weeping, sobbing in nearly soundless jerks of emotional agony, lost in a contrail of sensation and feeling she could neither identify a source for, nor make her own. *My blood is gone, it's become a thick gray river of frozen water, gone, all gone,* she thought insanely, and wave after wave of black tormented despair slapped her against the wall, hitting her like blows of living anger and pain. The landing above her was moving, expanding, flaming with a pulsing ugly light and then contracting like a diseased heart that laboured for strength.

Still and distant, Penny stood silhouetted against the moonlit window. Her face was chalky, her hair wild with an undefined electricity. The light took her in, enveloping and absorbing her, and as Jane watched in helpless weakness, she saw Penny's face change, as understanding and a kind of awareness flooded into it.

"Sing," Penny said, and the night took her voice and sent it echoing urgently, up and down the stairs. "Sing, Jane. Hurry, before she goes!"

There was something coming, bare inches from where Penny stood. It writhed and fought, as if the air through which it moved was solid, taking shape from the patches of darkness and light, struggling to form itself. Jane, fighting for control of her breathing, heard a thin reedy tenor from what seemed a great distance, and she knew that Ringan had heard Penny. Suddenly she understood what was needed.

Haltingly at first, she joined her voice to Ringan's.

"I am a hand-weaver to my trade," she quavered, *"I fell in love with a factory maid . . ."*

Air was coming back into her lungs now, and strength of voice with it. Ringan sounded stronger, too; she could tell, she could hear the difference.

"And if I could but her favour win, I'd stand beside her and weave by steam . . ."

She could not have moved from where she stood. The whole cottage seemed to be listening; the sense of surprise, of purpose suspended, was palpable in the charged air.

"My father to me scornful said, how could you fancy a factory maid . . ."

Ringan's voice came louder, startling and powerful. It rang out as if he held a microphone. *"When you could have girls fine and gay, dressed like unto the Queen of May?"*

The form that was not yet a solid thing strained toward them, yearning and aching. Why, Jane thought, she's not evil. She's not evil at all. She's just a girl in pain. The knowledge gave her strength, and she lifted her voice to match Ringan's, in perfect harmony.

"As for your fine girls, I don't care, if I could but enjoy my dear, I'd stand in the factory all the day, and she and I'd keep our shuttles in play."

On the landing, Penny stood and listened. She was not alone within herself. She was sharing body and mind; too much of the grief she felt, the passion, the anger and futility, and above all the brutal sense of loss, was tangibly not her own. Something was happening to the solid walls around her. She was here, but she was somewhere else as well, the stairs were wrong, they weren't there anymore, and the air around her was warm and cleanly sharp-scented, the darkness of a spring night out-of-doors, where apples grew and the river ran down to the sea.

And my body, she thought, that's shared too. There was pain, a horrible flame at the base of her neck, and she held something convulsively clutched in her hand, fabric, rough-spun yet comforting, she must lift it somehow, raise it up, and staunch this terrible fire in her throat, she must kill this pain before this pain killed her instead, but she couldn't, hand and cloth alike were too heavy, no movement was possible, and she was swallowing the hot coppery taste of blood . . .

Penny stood motionless, feeling everything that was her own and not her own. Betsy, she thought, oh, Betsy, you poor child, how did this happen to you, who did this? Tears began to slide down her cheeks, hot and salty. The shadow of not quite a girl fell across her feet. And all around her, from above and below, the pure tragic music went on.

"I went to my love's bedroom door, where often times I had been before, but I could not speak nor yet get in, the pleasant bed that my love lies in."

The third voice, when it came, was heard only by Penny. It was distant, despairing. It cut to the bone.

Will, oh Will, where are you, come to me then, you're hiding from me . . .

"How can you say it's a pleasant bed, when none lies there but a factory maid? Oh, a factory lass although she be, blessed is the man who would enjoy she."

Betsy was fading. Penny felt it, the weakening of that linked pain, the lessening of that sense of interior sharing, like a mother's touch removed. No, she thought, don't. Come back. Don't go, not yet, please.

"A pleasant thought's come to me mind, as I turned down the sheets so fine, and saw her two breasts standing so, like two white hills all covered with snow . . ."

Will?

They all heard it this time, the name of a young man untimely killed nearly two centuries earlier. The walls of Lumbe's seemed to sigh with a question, exhaling his name, letting it settle like dust on the shoulders of the living. Jane's voice caught, trembled, trailed off, and stopped. Above them, Ringan stilled his voice, letting the final lyrics of the verse fall away into silence.

Warmth flooded back into the cottage and into its occupants. For a moment, the sense and essence of Elizabeth Roper was there, undeniable, to feel and believe; warm, vital, a young girl who had worked too hard and loved too well and died before her death was due. The vagrant smell of lavender trembled through the air like a remembered kiss.

Then it was over.

Ringan got to Penny first, catching her as she swayed and collapsed at the knees. Jane, supporting herself with one hand on the stairwell wall, swallowed a lump in her throat as she saw the fierce protectiveness of Ringan's movements. He couldn't lift his lady; she was as tall as he and weighed nearly as much. Yet Jane knew that had it been possible, he would have picked Penny up like a child and carried her to her bed.

"Lavender," Jane said wonderingly. She moved up the stairs, moving slowly and limply. She crossed the landing and climbed the rest of the way, joining the others on the upper floor. "Did I smell lavender?"

"You did." Ringan had an arm around Penny's waist, and his free hand was brushing black hair away from her wet cheeks, touching her, reassuring himself that she was there and intact and somehow not taken from him. "Penny love, Penny lamb, you're all right. It's all right now."

"You're bloody well right about that, my love." She lifted her head and looked at them. Her eyes were blazing. "It is absolutely all right. I know what they both need, and I know how to give it to them. I know what we have to do."

"Good." Ringan's eyes were bright as well, and it was with an enormous sense of shock that Jane and Penny, seeing that look, realised that he was in a state of cold rage. "I'm very glad to hear it. You just tell me what you think the dear dead thing wants from you. Because I've had about enough of this rubbish."

The triumphant light in Penny's eyes died. "Ringan . . ."

"No." Angry, warlike breath whistled through his nostrils. He moved back and locked his look to hers. "Don't you give me my own name, and don't you hand me soft words either. Christ, Penny, are you completely oblivious to what's happening here? From the first moment you came across them, that first bit of music you heard, you've been like a half-starved rose wanting a taste of sunlight—it's like you're addicted to these bloody ghosts!"

She said nothing.

Jane, moving back into shadow and trying to make herself invisible, thought she had never seen anything as blank, as quiet, as Penny's face. Ringan, his anger and fear irrationally fanned by her lack of response, took Penny by the shoulders and gave her a single hard shake.

"You're doing it now, do you realise that? It's as if you'd like nothing better than to run off into the ether and play with the spooks. D'ye think I can't see what's happening? They're sucking you in, pulling you away. If we don't get them out of here, there'll be nothing left of you!" He finally heard his own voice, shouting at the top of his considerable range. It dropped to a broken whisper. "And I'm damned if I'll let that happen. I'll burn this place to the ground first."

Penny, immobile throughout his outburst, suddenly moved. She raised a hand and brought it to rest against his cheek.

"You don't have to burn it down," she told him. A smile broke across her face, a smile that was present, and aware, and completely her own. She saw the muscles in Ringan's throat working. "That's what she showed me, Ringan. I know what we have to do to end it."

On Sunday morning, Ringan tried to phone Albert Wychsale and found that the phones were off.

"Damn." He dangled the receiver loosely in one hand, a picture of frustration and disgust. "The wind must have blown some of the lines down. We're having no luck, are we? Now what do we do?"

"We'll have to drive up there." Penny, who had braved the muddy garden to gather herbs, pushed the kitchen doors shut. Her dark hair was glossy, spangled like a gypsy's scarf with droplets of rain. After the events of the night before, it was odd that all three felt so energised, so rested. Penny, in particular, looked vibrant, as if she had returned from a long holiday in a warm languid place. Betsy Roper's communication had left no scars at all. "God, it's like Noah's revenge out there."

"There's no real rush, is there?" Jane took the herbs from Penny, found saucers in the cupboard, and began sorting through the dark leaves with the practised speed of a true gardener. "Thyme, chives . . . I mean, if you can't call your noble patron, then we can't call Liam or Matty, either. If you'd just get yourself into the twenty-first century and succumb to the lure of technology . . ."

"Yes, I know, I'd have a functional cell phone and we wouldn't be having this problem. Thanks ever so much for that cheerful thought," Ringan said gloomily. "Shame the battery on yours ran down. Anyway, if we can't find out what happened to that little toy you both saw Will Corby fondling, we're going to have to do some hard thinking. But I hate putting this off. It's all tricky enough as it is. I want to get it done, get it over. I want those damned ghosts out of my house and out of my barn and out of my life, and to have to delay because of the weather . . ."

"Don't fuss, darling. We'll cope." There was a deep tenderness in Penny's tone. "However long it takes, we'll cope. Here, have some breakfast. Everything seems more difficult on an empty stomach."

"Amen to that," Jane mumbled through a mouthful of food. Conversation was suspended, the only sounds for a few minutes being due to the steady ingestion of breakfast and the occasional clatter of cutlery.

Jane was the first to finish. She set her fork down, looking thoughtful.

"Ringan," she began, "you spent lots of time up at the manor house, right? Do you remember coming across anything about a collection, or a museum, or anything of that nature?"

"Wychsale family history, you mean?"

"Well, no, not exactly." Jane struggled to organise her thoughts. "Actually, I'm thinking more about Betsy, about her job. She seems to respond so strongly to that song, and Will Corby does too. And this Will bloke was obviously a weaver—I mean, we're not arguing on that score, are we? No? Good, I thought not. Where I'm going with this—well, the lyrics are awfully specific. Didn't you say something, back in Padstow, about the Wychsales expanding their holdings with a textile mill, during the last century?"

"Yes, I—oh, my Lord." Ringan looked at Penny, and shook his

head at his own obtuseness. "We have been dim bulbs, haven't we, pet?"

"If you say so." Penny touched a napkin to her lips. "Would you mind telling me what you're talking about?"

"Piers Wychsale. The Right Hon's worthy ancestor." Ringan set his cup down and stared at them. "You asked about him, remember? And I said at least some members of Lumbe's original family probably worked at the Wychsale textile mill—it was downriver, a very profitable family concern for about forty years."

"What happened to it?" Jane asked. "Is it still operating, after all this time? And does it have a museum?"

Ringan shook his head. "The mill's been gone forever; it closed down around the time Dickens was in full swing. The building suffered heavy structural damage during a spring flood, I remember that, and the family didn't want to spend the lolly doing the necessary repairs. It was demolished, I think sometime around the Crimean War. And our Betsy—the factory maid?"

Jane said eagerly, "So you think Betsy Roper worked for the Wychsale of her time?"

"Of course she did! As for a collection . . ." Ringan drew in a deep breath, and continued triumphantly, "There is most definitely a collection. Not of the Wychsale family, but of the mill. I know just where it is, too."

"Break it to us gently." Penny's dryness hid her own surge of excitement, a feeling the hunter gets when, after a long day of false scents, he at last picks up a legitimate spoor. "We can't bear the suspense."

"Glastonbury." Ringan was on his feet. "The Abbey Barn in Glastonbury proper. The place houses something called the Somerset Rural Life Museum. And there's a whole room devoted to the history of the textile industry in the county. I've never actually been all the way upstairs to that particular section, but I've heard it's a superb collection."

"What are we waiting for?" Penny abandoned what was left of her toast and tea, and grabbed for her handbag. "Let's get on!"

It had stopped raining, and a clean, sharp wind was blowing.

They piled into the Jaguar, Penny glaring at the wet leaves blown by the storm across the car's bonnet. She worried briefly about Butterball, whom they had found in the kitchen in the morning, curled tight between the cooker and the fridge, having made himself as small as such a large cat could. He had still been shaken, refusing to remain in the house even after an offer of milk, streaking out of Lumbe's the moment the garden door had been opened for him. Penny consoled herself with the specialist survival skills of felines as a breed, and turned the car toward the road to Glastonbury.

The country roads bore telling evidence of the night's stormy weather. They saw trees down, more than one of them bearing the ugly, unmistakable charring that showed where lightning had taken them. Plowed fields were muddy and unrecognisable, fenced allotments showed only the tops of lovingly tended cabbages under pools of rainwater. Wet leaves were everywhere, and the storm-pocked road surfaces made for bumpy driving, even with the Jaguar's superb system of shocks and struts. Many of the district's apple trees, laden with late spring fruit, had been stripped bare. As Ringan remarked, if he'd had a cider press to go with his eighteenth-century cottage, he could have gathered enough windfalls to keep even such a prodigious drinker as Liam McCall drunk on sour makeshift cider for a month or two.

As they approached Glastonbury, they caught sight of Glastonbury Tor, fabulous against the sky. If the night's heavy weather had touched it, nothing could be seen of damage; the ancient building, dark-stoned and stark, stood as it had done for time out of mind. Above it, soft white clouds scudded and played, seeming to wreath the black finger of stone with a vaporous halo.

Penny remembered what Albert Wychsale had said about the Tor being a magnet for storms and disturbances. A picture popped into her head, sourceless, unaccountable, irrelevant: Lumbe's tithe barn, wisps of smoke forcing their delicate inexorable way through holes burning in the upper walls, hungry cat's tongues of flame streaking the massive beams, eating away at anything that fire might find to burn. The picture was vivid, and bright. She shuddered, and the car swerved slightly.

"Something wrong, love?" Ringan had caught that tiny, quickly controlled twitch. She shook her head, threw him a brief smile, and pulled hurriedly to the left as Ringan's pointing finger shot out.

"There it is, there's the Abbey Barn. Here, Pen, just pull into the car park."

There were only a few cars scattered throughout the lot; either the museum hadn't opened yet, Ringan thought, or else the threat of more unfriendly weather to come was keeping the inevitable flock of tourists away. They bought their admission tickets— Ringan, despite his National Trust membership, was a firm believer in paying cash for the good of the monuments the Trust had been created to preserve—and made a beeline for the barn's huge doors.

The first sight of the old building's vast interior brought the two women to an abrupt stop. Penny, taller by far than Jane, moved to one side and let Jane gape. Even Ringan, who had seen it several times before, paused for a moment to gaze upward in deep appreciation.

"My God." Jane, craning her neck toward the barn's shadowy, vaulted heights, drew a deep breath. "That's the most astonishing thing I have ever seen."

"You can say that?" Ringan teased. "After what you've seen at Lumbe's? No, I'm joking. It's really incredible, isn't it? This is called a two-tiered crucked roof, and believe me, it's every bit as solid as it looks. This is why I've never made it all the way upstairs, to check out the exhibits; I mean to, I swear I do, but every time I've walked in here, I've just stood here and gawked. See those huge cross beams? Every one of them was carved out of a single tree trunk."

"I believe it." Penny's eyes travelled the length of the barn's sombre, stone-walled magnificence. "Now, this is what I call a proper tithe barn. It looks like some enormous venerable uncle to your barn, Ringan. I can't believe that ceiling! How old is it, anyway?"

"What, the roof? Fourteenth century, I think." Ringan let them absorb the place, with its soaring roof and cross-shaped slit windows, for a few moments. "It's, what, about six times the size of my little bit of barn? Eight times? Damnation, I do believe I'm having an attack of tithe barn envy. Come on, ladies, we've got work to do. Let's get a move on."

They found the room devoted to Somerset's history with textiles near the top of the museum, after some unplanned stops along the way. Penny, examining the pitiful artifacts of a woman who had died at the local workhouse in abject poverty and been buried by the parish, expended some stinging eloquence on the inequities of the ancient class structure. Jane wandered ahead and was found in rapt contemplation of a pair of woman's shoes, cut and stitched by hand two centuries earlier. And Ringan, who was of them all the most impatient, fell in love with a massive nineteenth-century cider press and had to be dragged forcibly away from it. At length, they came to the final rooms of exhibits.

"Aha!" Ringan hurried in first. "Never let it be said that a Scotsman ever forgets a trivial fact. Here we go, ladies. Welcome to the Glastonbury Stores. Second floor, textiles, local history, ladies' lingerie . . ."

"Ringan?" Jane's voice was so intense that they both swivelled round to stare at her. "Look at this. I do believe we've found the promised land."

Mounted carefully inside two squares of glass, stretched to its full existing width of just over a meter square, was the end of their search.

"It's here." Penny sounded stunned. "Do you know, I don't think I believed it ever really existed? But it's here."

After seeing Will Corby's love gift through the veil of a temporal mist, the genuine item was a shock, at once less intense and more immediately impactive than its noncorporeal twin. It was not intact, having lost a large section from the lower left corner to some past catastrophe. The colours were both cruder and more defined than their ghostly counterparts. Time had not played well with what remained of the cloth, fraying the edges, showing the joins in the weave. A carelessly woven cloud along the topmost edge showed where the moths had found it.

But Betsy Roper was there, a small figure of a girl, lovingly executed with an exaggeratedly tiny waist and a floating lively cloud of black hair. She held one hand out to not quite rest on the trunk of an apple tree, woven with rough, yet lively red fruit dotting the green of the canopy. Beside her, done with no care to proportion or depth, but sporting its chimney stack, was a small cottage.

"It's Lumbe's," Ringan said. His voice was so flat and dry that Penny understood he was very much moved, on the edge of tears. "Look. There's only one level, but it's Lumbe's."

"There's blood on it." Jane stretched out the tip of her index finger. Beside her, Penny had begun to tremble. Looking at the rusty brown stain smeared across the upper edge of the tapestry somehow made Betsy Roper more real than she had been to either of them. "See? There, in the upper left corner. That's blood, isn't it? Betsy's blood." She added, very softly, "Oh, God. Poor Betsy. How did her blood get on it?"

"You don't know it's Betsy's." Penny sounded shaken, and her voice lacked conviction. "It mightn't even be blood."

"Half a second, will you? Here's a card." Ringan, his nose half an inch from the glass, read it aloud. "Right, here we go: 'From the private collection of Sir James Bedbere, magistrate, donated 1842. Hand-woven tapestry coverlet, circa 1817. Made by William Corby, a hand-weaver from Street, as a gift to the girl he had apparently hoped to marry, Elizabeth Roper of Glastonbury. The coverlet was used only once, by Elizabeth's mother, to cover her daughter's body on the floor of her family's cottage, after the girl was stabbed in the neck by her brother George and staggered indoors to die.' "

"Oh, Jesus," Jane whispered. "I knew it. Betsy's blood."

Ringan, squinting, read on. " 'William Corby, the second victim of Glastonbury's May Day double homicide in 1817, was a salutory example of what drove the adherents of the Luddite doctrine to their fabled extremes. The Corby family, prosperous yeoman hand-weavers for generations, had lost much of their custom after the Right Honourable Piers Wychsale opened his textile mill in 1807.' "

Ringan's voice died away. In the silence that followed, the old barn seemed to settle around them. Outside, it had begun to rain again.

"Those poor kids," Penny said finally. "Killed by Betsy's brother. Ringan, I found George Roper's name, when I found the family in the Wychsale register for the early 1790s. Remember? We were surprised there were just the two children."

"I do remember, yes. We need more information. The May Day murders?" Ringan frowned, his eyebrows drawn into a single line of concentration. "I don't think I've ever heard of them."

"We can find out, can't we? I mean, that bit's simple enough." Jane touched the display case lightly. "The public library, police records, the newspaper accounts of the time. There must have been a lot of local coverage. I wonder if anyone's written them up, in the modern age, I mean?"

"True," Ringan agreed. "And if worse comes to worst, there's always the muniment room up at Wychsale House. You realise, don't you, that this confirms something quite amazing? We really have been seeing and hearing and feeling all the things we thought we'd been seeing. We're not mental. And that poor bloke out in the barn, he really did communicate with Jane."

"Will Corby," Jane said complacently. "I told you he'd given me his name."

"One of the strangest introductions in history." Penny spoke lightly, but her mouth wanted to tremble. "And that poor girl at Lumbe's, Betsy Roper. I wonder why her brother went for them. Do you suppose he thought this was some wealthy nob taking advantage of a working-class girl? Or that perhaps he simply wasn't quite right in the head? Or—oh, what a beastly idea to get— maybe he wanted her himself? Or—or what?"

"Let's go find out. Oh, damn!" Ringan, turning toward the stairs, halted in his tracks. "We're forgetting the other half of all this. Is there any sign of that toy handloom thing?"

"I've already looked. The answer is no." Penny headed for the stairs. "We're on a bit of a roll, aren't we? Long may the luck hold. Where to first, Ringan?"

"Library. They're sure to have a section on local history, probably with newspaper copies."

"And since you're a member in good standing of the National Trust, our way in is already properly greased." They reached the ground floor and sprinted for the Jaguar as a flurry of storm clouds spattered them with rain. Weeping weather, Penny thought. "Ringan, wait a bit. I've just had a sickening thought. Is the local library open on Sunday?"

"It doesn't matter." Jane, seeing the dawning dismay in Ringan's eyes, interposed quickly. "Yesterday, when I was wondering about town, I passed at least two bookshops on the High Street. One of them looked absolutely perfect."

"You're right." Penny released the handbrake, backed the car in a fast, expert, three-point turn, and merged onto the road toward town. "I know which one you mean. Very much slanted for the scholarly or pseudo-scholarly tourist, complete with lots of little privately published pamphlets about King Arthur and the history of UFO sightings up at the Tor. Right?"

"That's the one. About thirty steps up the hill from that Tudor-looking hotel or pub or whatever it is." The Jaguar turned into Magdalene Road; Penny drove slowly, her eyes peeled for a parking slot, aware of the looming ruin of Glastonbury Abbey casting towering shadows to their right. She saw a parking spot, twisted the car into place, and jumped out.

"Up the hill." Ringan fumbled in his pockets for a coin, then remembered it was Sunday. "Come on."

The girl behind the counter was, in herself, a good advertisement for the bookshop's speciality. She was small, plump, and swathed from chin to ankles in a deliberately arts-and-crafts selection of badly matched homespuns, of the type that Ringan privately thought of as Ye Olde Ragbag. Her hair, which genetics had meant to be inoffensive brown, was streaked with red and black; it dangled down her back in a profusion of skinny plaits. On the front of the amorphous garment that draped her shoulders was a large badge. It sported a drawing of a broomstick, surrounded by the legend "Glastonbury: Love It Or I'll Turn You Into A Toad!"

"Good grief," Penny muttered under her breath. Jane flashed her a look and bit back on a grin. It was amazing, Jane thought how much more like their usual selves they were, away from the cottage and barn.

"Good morning. May I help you?" The girl's accents were pure Somerset.

"I hope so." Ringan's eyes were already scanning the shelves, picking out subject headers. "We need whatever you've got on something called the May Day murders. Historical, happened in 1817. The people involved were called Roper and Corby."

"May first, 1817, actually." The girl bustled out from behind the cash register. "A sad, sad story, that was. A pair of young lovers, surprised by the girl's brother. He was hanged for it, you know. Here we go, local history, nineteenth century. Now let me see—I've got two collections that feature the case, and one small pamphlet devoted entirely to it."

"I'll take all three." Ringan did a sum in his head, pulled out the appropriate cash, and followed the girl back to the counter. "Ta."

"Ta to you too," the girl said cheerily, "and may the goddess stand at your shoulder."

Twenty minutes later, back at Lumbe's, they divided Ringan's purchases among them, perched on the sofa, and began to read. Penny, who had chosen a slim, elegant volume with the imposing title *Farms, Fabrics and Freeholds: Post-Industrial Revolution Life Among Somerset's Working Classes,* checked the index, found what she was looking for, and finished first.

"Right." She laid the book down. "Your attention, please, lady and gent. I've got some gen for you. May first, 1817. Victim number one, Elizabeth Roper, aged eighteen, employed at the Wychsale textile mill, so there's two points for our Ringan. This was definitely our Betsy. Apparently the eldest of an appallingly oversized family, which by the way answers our questions about a labouring family with only two offspring. They must have dropped a few more litters in the intervening years. But the one that counts would be Betsy's brother George, called Georgie. Not quite two years younger than his sister. Big and strong, and"—she tapped the book with one finger—"if this is anything to go by, a bit of a lout, even before the killings."

"My historian agrees with yours. Lout is the word, all right." Ringan lifted his eyes from the printed page he'd been devouring, and slipped a finger between the pages to hold his place. "I've just found him, as well. He seems to have been an unstable mixture of unfortunate qualities, our Georgie; hot-tempered, sullen, thick as a brick . . ."

"Muddled," Jane chimed in. They turned to stare at her. "Resentful in a dull, unspecific sort of way. Angry about every-thing, general anger really, but especially class anger. The most dangerous type, always smouldering away. Also, I get the feeling he had other things percolating, especially insofar as his sister was concerned. Rather ugly, really, and it's not made any prettier by the fact that he likely had no clue about those other things."

The others stared at her. She went on, rather dreamily. "I suspect Betsy was some sort of symbol to him, at the very least, though heaven only knows of what. Purity, the working classes sullied by the upper classes?" She considered a moment. "I wonder why these books always seem to find the killer more interesting than the victims? There's nearly a whole page about him, and only a para-graph each about Betsy and her weaver lad. I suppose it's because the killer's there, you know? The victims have to be reconstructed, they can't speak for themselves." She looked regretful.

"Weaver lad?" Penny had focused on the facts, and her mouth curved into a satisfied smile. "Then he was definitely a weaver? All doubts removed, one hundred percent certain and for sure? How nice to be right."

"A hand-weaver, just as the card at the museum said, and just as what seems to be his favourite tune says. 'I am a hand-weaver to my trade.' Like father, like son, and like four or five generations of Corby men before them." Ringan sounded sad. "Mine's got a good two pages on the trial itself, and it's enough to make you want to curl up in a corner and go foetal. Talk about Romeo and bleeding Juliet! I'll tell you what, if this book's not completely apocryphal, the whole world got in Betsy and Will's way, and I do mean the whole world; their families, their circumstances, the social economics of the day. The poor brats were doomed from day one. This is pitiful."

Penny stretched her legs, wriggled her feet, and with a sigh of satisfaction listened to her own ankles pop. "Tell us more."

"I was planning to. Betsy worked at the mill, which was taking away Corby Senior's business and destroying a family tradition into the bargain. So Will's papa wouldn't have been too fond of the girl. And of course, the Corbys were yeoman class, not labourers. Then there's Betsy's endless family, or should I say tribe? If she was the eldest, with a good steady-paying job, you can bet her people weren't about to let that vital source of income go off with a lusty boy from Street."

"And if you drop her fire-eating, to-hell-with-the-nobs brother into the kettle, you've got a Greek tragedy looking for someone to happen to," Penny said slowly. "It all sounds so damnably familiar. Euripides, or Sophocles, would find this story inevitable. What exactly did happen, Ringan? It's time we knew as much of the story as there is."

"Apparently, there was the usual May Day fete being held in Glastonbury. It's an annual tradition, crafts and meat pies and Hobby Horses and girls with ribbons, the whole May Day lot. Goes back for centuries—here, let me read it to you." He picked up the book, opened it, and cleared his throat. " 'During the murder trial of George Roper, the testimony of Will Corby's sister Jane and the Roper family made clear that Elizabeth and Will must have been meeting clandestinely every Friday night for some months prior to the events of 1 May. Under examination, the Wychsale family's head groom, Michael Dailey, admitted that he had attempted to attach Elizabeth's favours, but had been rebuffed. He further deposed that motivated by malice toward Elizabeth and a feeling of frustrated conceit, he had teased George Roper about his sister's Friday night trysting. Dailey, who swore that he had not considered what action, if any, his words might provoke on the part of George Roper, was reprimanded by the magistrate in charge . . . ' "

"What a swine," Jane said through her teeth. "What a bloody-minded little tick. I wish they'd castrated him. Hell, I hope they lynched him, the spiteful vicious stoat."

"Well, I don't know about that, but there is a footnote about him being turned off from his job at the manor. If there's any justice in this world, maybe he starved to death. I'm with you—what a mean little bastard." Ringan scanned the page. "Where was I? Ah. 'George Roper, his suspicions aroused, said that he had confronted Elizabeth with Dailey's accusations, and that his sister, who was a spirited girl, had slapped his face and told him that she would not tolerate him prying into her business or concerns . . . ' "

"Good on Betsy," Penny said approvingly. "I'm beginning to like the girl."

"So am I, weirdly enough; I just don't want her in my house anymore. But let's get to the meat of it." Ringan read rapidly, turned the page, and grunted with satisfaction. "Here we go. 'On the night of 1 May, Elizabeth offered to take two of her younger siblings to Glastonbury, so that they might enjoy the dancing and fireworks. She invited George to accompany them, with the understanding that George would bring the children home in good time, should Elizabeth choose to remain late at the celebrations. George, agreeing to this arrangement, accompanied them. After walking some distance toward Glastonbury, the family was offered a lift in a pony cart—' " Ringan stopped, and made a noise in his throat. "Well, I'll be damned!"

"That's as may be," Jane said. "Ringan, what is it?"

" ' . . . offered a lift in a pony cart,' " he read slowly and clearly, " 'driven by Will Corby.' "

There was a deep silence as they digested this. The old tragedy seemed very clear, almost present. With the image of a tiny woven girl on a bloodied cloth fresh in their minds, the comfortable room held old emotional echoes. To the two women, who had both seen the physical wraith of Will Corby, it was almost too vivid. Penny remembered the compact strength of Will's shoulders. She thought of the broad, workingman's fingers with their callused tips, the hands that had woven that picture of his darling girl. She remembered, too, how tenderly they had smoothed the bed of hay that had supported Betsy Roper's vital young body, and swallowed hard.

"Go on, Ringan," Jane said quietly. Penny looked at her and saw her own feelings reflected in Jane's eyes. "Go on, finish it. How did it happen? The mechanics of the crime, I mean?"

" 'George Roper said that nothing beside commonplaces passed between his sister and Corby during the drive into Glastonbury to make him suspect that Will Corby might be the man involved with Elizabeth. Nevertheless, he had already formed the belief that his sister planned to meet her unknown lover that evening. He determined to keep her under his eye, while trying as best he could to appear normal in his manner to her.' "

He paused, letting the women absorb the mental pictures: the cunning but unstable adolescent, plotting and scheming. What had been in his mind, Ringan wondered, and continued to read.

" 'Sometime after eight o'clock, the cart reached Glastonbury. Will Corby tethered his pony cart, accepted thanks for his kindness in offering the Roper family a lift, and went off on his own. Nothing could be firmly established as to his movements between that time and the tragic events of shortly before midnight. Although not established by testimony,' " Ringan read, " 'it is probable that arrangements were made between Elizabeth and Will, to meet after the fete had ended. While no one living could attest with certainty as to when or how that meeting was arranged, Mary Roper, aged eight, said that she and her brothers had crowded into the rear of the cart, while Elizabeth sat up front with Corby. It is probable that the lovers took this opportunity to arrange or confirm their meeting after the fete at an old tithe barn, situated a short distance from the Roper cottage on the banks of the Carlyon. The barn is part of the Wychsale demesne.' "

" 'While no one living could attest . . . ' " Penny's eyes were filmed with the weight of unshed tears. Ringan sent her a soft look, and continued.

" 'Shortly after ten, the fireworks display ended. Jack and Mary Roper were both sleepy, and Elizabeth suggested that her brother take the children home, as agreed upon earlier. She may have assumed that they would be forced to walk, thereby arriving home at a late hour. However, a farmer stopped and offered them a lift almost immediately upon their setting foot on the road to Street.' "

"All right." Jane's eyebrows had drawn together. "So she figured Georgie would get home late, with two exhausted kids fussing and being demanding, the way kids do, and that would keep him busy. She knew she had a ride waiting. It must have seemed perfect, except for one thing. If she was banking on the timing, wouldn't she have figured out the danger?"

"You mean, that Will's pony cart would pass her brothers and sister on the road home?" Penny was thinking hard. "No. There are other roads Will could have taken, not as direct. It should have been easy enough to avoid the younger Ropers. All they had to do was keep off the main road, and Georgie was sure to take that one. Betsy and Will were both locals, and it seemed they'd been meeting on the QT for a goodish time. They must have known every hedge and stile in the county." She glanced at Ringan, who had been reading silently. "Can you summarise it for us, love? Or are all the details vital to what we need?"

"No, they're not. Right, I'll sum up." The judge's ancient phrase sounded odd on his lips. "Georgie got the kids home in half an hour; the kindly farmer dropped them at their door. A staggering bit of bad luck for Betsy and Will, that Samaritan was—lethal, in fact. If they'd had to walk, or at least had to wait for a ride home, the tragedy likely wouldn't have happened that night. As it was, Georgie got the kids indoors, helped his mother get them settled, and said he was keyed up and was going for a walk. He said at the trial he didn't go far, but he must have gone far enough in the wrong direction to have missed Betsy and Will. They left Glaston-bury in Will's pony cart at half past ten and got to Lumbe's right around eleven. Will left the cart under some trees, not two hundred yards from Lumbe's, and that's where Georgie found it at half past eleven. Georgie tracked them to the tithe barn, and found his sister with her weaver. Fifteen minutes later, Will Corby was dead, drowned in the Carlyon with his head held under the water. Betsy bled to death on the cottage floor. She'd been stabbed in the neck, trying to keep her brother from killing her lover."

Eight

The loom goes click and the loom goes clack
The shuttle flies forward and then flies back
The weaver's so bent that he's like to crack
Such a wearisome trade is the weaver's

"Liam? Is that you? Are you awake?"

"Mrmph." The indistinct gurgle might have meant anything: acknowledgment, rage, a simple snore. Damn, Jane thought. I need him awake, and he sounds hung over. "Liam?"

"Yes, Jane, I'm still Liam. I was Liam when you woke me up a moment ago, and I'm still Liam. What do you want?"

"We need you. Can you come here?"

"Bloody hell. Wait a bit, can you?" Mercifully, he set the phone aside and, after apparently rummaging around and finding a tissue, spent the next minute in as extensive a clearing-out of sinuses as Jane, listening with a kind of horrified wonder, had ever heard. That attended to, Liam took up the phone again. "All right, that's better. Jane?"

"Here. Still here."

"Good. You need me, you say, and can I come there? Why do you need me, who is 'we' and where is 'here'?"

Jane glanced up and made eye contact with Ringan, who was watching her expectantly. It had been Ringan's idea for Jane to call Liam, since in his view, the prickly fiddler was less likely to prove intractable with Jane than with either of his male band mates. Now that she had Liam on the phone, however, the idea no longer seemed a good one; in fact, leaving her to deal with Liam before he was fully awake seemed not only cheeky and a bit mean, but selfish as well. Jane made a mental note to hit Ringan once, fairly hard, when their business was concluded, and turned her attention back to the phone.

"Right," he was saying crossly. "Wake me up, ask a favour, and then swallow your own vocal cords. Bloody rude, I call it. Jane! Pay attention and talk to me. Where? Why?"

"Ringan's new place. For a concert in his little bit of tithe barn. No audience, no money; just come, will you? You're wanted." Jane considered a moment, decided it needed more, and added, "Oh—right, why. To get rid of a ghost, well, two ghosts. I mean, hopefully, to get rid of two ghosts."

Silence, which went on far too long for Jane's peace of mind. She was aware of how peculiar her explanation had been. A speechless Liam was unnerving. "Liam?"

"Liam indeed. Still the one and only. Jane, dear," he said conversationally, "you do realise, don't you, me darlin' girl, that if you're having me on, and you drag me down to the back of wherever on a joke or a whim or an I-don't-know-what, I'll have to kill you? Beat you to death with your own flute? This is something you know, right, love?"

"It's not a joke, damn it, it's an exorcism! And it's not the back of wherever, it's just outside the town of Street, near Glastonbury, in the grand old County of Somerset." Jane, spurred by desperation, had a sudden burst of brilliance. "You know, Liam, this is the best cider country anywhere. Real cider. West Country cider."

"Cider? Why didn't you say so, and save me wasting all this time arguing?" He sounded genuinely irritated. "Right, I'm in. On my way. I'll drive. When am I wanted?"

"We want to do this tomorrow afternoon—soonest is best on this. And it ought to be done in daylight. Here, talk to Ringan; he'll tell you the route."

Jane handed Ringan the phone and let her breath out in a long, heartfelt exhale. She caught Penny's sympathetic eye.

"Oh, dear. Was he being a menace?"

"Oddly enough, not very much. Just—being Liam. Next time, Ringan gets to prod the bear and I get to call Matty." She turned as Ringan hung up. "Ringan, is he coming?"

"He is. And Matty, as well, bless his heart. Matty didn't even ask why we needed him, just right, what's the way down, anything you need me to bring, see you tomorrow. He's a good bloke." Ringan ran one hand through his hair; he managed to sound both distracted and concentrated. "So we've set the gears moving. God, I hope this works. If it doesn't . . ."

"Good morning."

They all jumped. Albert Wychsale had come up the garden path and poked his head in through the kitchen's Dutch doors.

"My word, you all look a bit like stuffed owls. Sorry; I didn't mean to startle you."

"Albert, come in, come in, do do do. You're just the man we want right now." Penny pulled the Right Hon unceremoniously into the kitchen. Sunlight streaked the walls, and edged Penny's hair momentarily with a bright nimbus of light. The storm had passed, presumably making its way south toward the Channel and Normandy. In its wake were three counties full of downed trees, scattered summer produce, and muddy roads, interspersed with broken power lines and damaged property. "I'm glad you're here. We tried calling you yesterday, but the wretched phones were very uncooperative, and they've only just come back on this morning. How did you know we wanted to see you?"

"Flattering." He bobbed his head at Penny, but his eyes were on Jane. "Most flattering, but truth to tell, it never even occurred to me. I happened to be out checking the storm damage and thought I'd see how Lumbe's had weathered the weather, so to speak. Is all well?"

"I think so. I mean, we haven't been up on the roof or anything, but no signs of leaks. This place is remarkably sturdy, isn't it? I'm not certain anything short of a tactical nuclear missile would really damage it. Your family certainly knew how to build labourer's hovels, back in the good old days." Penny took note of the admiration and curiosity on Wychsale's face. "Oh, dear—where have my manners gone begging? Albert, may I introduce Jane Castle? She's a flutist and vocalist, and a member of Ringan's band. Jane, allow me to present to you the Right Honourable Albert Wychsale, the current Baron Boult. I can see by the look in his eye that he's about to wave off the tired upper-class ancestral formalities yoked so heavily about his neck by generations of mouldy old familial inheritance, and insist that you call him Albert. Aren't you, Albert?"

"Naughty." Wychsale was grinning. "But quite right, as it happens, I am. This is lovely, Jane. Please do call me Albert."

"Oh—right, you're Ringan's landlord. Very nice to meet you, Albert." Jane offered a hand. "You've got an amazing cat, did you know? And this is a really lovely bit of property you've given Ringan, even with the ghosts."

The smile faded. "Ah yes, the ghosts. Lumbe's unidentified purveyors of clammy skin and bad dreams. Any progress on that?"

"Progress? Yes indeed. For one thing, they aren't unidentified anymore. We've put names to them." Ringan handed Wychsale a cup. "In fact, they're famous, although not as ghosts. Did you ever hear of the May Day murders? First of May, 1817?"

"No, I don't think—oh, wait. Now I think of it, I believe I have, vaguely. I seem to remember coming across a mention of it years ago, in the family muniments, I think. Weren't they a pair of young lovers, or something? Killed by a family member? I believe one of the victims, the girl, actually worked at our family's factory—" Ringan saw the sudden realisation dawn in Wychsale's face. "Oh, dear Lord. At the family factory indeed. Are you sure this is them?"

"Yes." Jane's face was suddenly shadowed and pinched. "We are. Quite sure."

"Well." Wychsale, seemingly at a loss for words, sipped his tea. "Any ideas about it? As in, coping with the situation?"

Ringan exchanged a meaningful look with the two women, "As it happens . . ."

"You *do*? Yes, I can see you do. But that's splendid!"

"I hope so," Ringan said slowly. "Because it occurs to me that if this doesn't work, we'll be left completely at a loss. I mean, this is rather an 'all or nothing at all' sort of exorcism we're talking about. If this program won't fly as planned, we've got nothing at all. And if I can't get them out, I can't live here, nor can Penny. So it has to work."

Wychsale looked around for a seat, found nothing, and perched gingerly on the edge of the Dutch door. "An exorcism. Yes, that would follow, wouldn't it? I suppose, being a good Church of England chap, I can't be blamed for not thinking of it before. What have you got in mind?"

"A concert," Ringan explained. "A show, strictly private. I'll give you all of it later, the how and why we got to this idea, but for now, here's the gist: we've got a dead yeoman weaver and his dead labouring-class factory girl, and they both respond to a particular piece of music. I'm not at all surprised, by the way; the lyric might just as well have been written about what happened to them, in their lives. They used to meet in the tithe barn—that's in all the trial transcripts, and it explains the young man, Will Corby his name was, and why he's stuck in the barn. So we're going to have this little do in the barn, play the song, and hope for the best."

"Did he die in the barn?" Wychsale was fascinated. "Was he killed in there? I mean, I would have thought it would be one of the great family historical dinner table stories, having a barn that was a murder site. And I've never heard a word about it."

"No, he was held down and drowned in the stream, by the girl's awful little brother. As for the girl herself . . ."

"Wait a bit," Penny broke in. "Back up a bit, Ringan. There's a reason we've been trying to call you since yesterday, Albert. There's something we think would absolutely cinch a successful exorcism, and we can't find it, and we were hoping you might know where it is. A little carved model of a handloom, toy-sized really. Carved in wood."

Wychsale was frowning. "A toy wooden handloom?"

"It was a token, we think." Jane moved out from the shadows and into a patch of warm sunlight. "A love gift, from the girl—her name was Elizabeth Roper, by the way—to Will Corby. I've seen Will in the barn, up close and personal; he's actually spoken to me, in a manner of speaking. Penny's seen him, as well. And both times, he's been carrying that wooden toy, cradling it really. It's obviously got some special importance to him. There's a second token as well, a gift from Will to Betsy Roper, that's actually a sort of tapestry picture of her, but it's tucked between two nice thick sheets of glass in the Somerset Rural Life Museum, and we can't get at it. So . . ."

"Yes. Yes, I see." Wychsale was up and moving. "You feel the presence of at least one of these items would be, what, a focal point, a way to summon him there? So that you can send him off to, well, wherever it is ghosts go?" He paused for a moment, and added thoughtfully, "Do you know, I hope that if they actually go somewhere after an exorcism, it's somewhere rather nice. Being stuck as a half-shaped memory in a bit of ether for years, perhaps centuries—I call that a very bad joke to have played on you. And if you were rather a nice person to begin with, then I'd say adding the fear factor to it, always having to terrify other people when you mean no harm at all and never did, is really a bit too much, all around."

"That's exactly right—everything you just said, I mean." Ringan eyed Wychsale with respect, and some surprise. From the beginning, for a pampered upper-class son of the British gentry, the Right Hon had displayed an unusual streak of sensitivity and openmindedness. Perhaps it was due to his boyhood one-on-one with Elizabeth Roper's chilly, grieving essence on the stairs at Lumbe's, but whatever the cause, it was unusual and laudable. "And yes, of course, we want to put him and his lady love to eternal rest, in the best possible way. I'll think about where the eternal rest might happen, not to mention who's offering rooms at the inn, another day; this is a bit too much for a practising agnostic to cope with in one afternoon. What I really want is to get them out of here. I'm not comfortable having them in my home, or in my life."

"So I'd imagine." Wychsale was looking businesslike. "May I use your phone? I don't have my cell phone with me, and I want to call John Wainfleet. If anyone knows where this wooden model thing might be, it would be he."

Luckily, the Wychsale librarian was at home. The conversation was concise and to the point: Wainfleet had no knowledge of the artifact in question, but he would spend his day trying to track it down. Yes, he had several sources to whom he might turn. No, it was absolutely no trouble. Certainly, he understood the need for haste; deadlines, after all, were deadlines.

"That's splendid, John. Can you call Ringan Laine at Lumbe's with any news? You have the number, don't you? Right, then. Thanks, John." Wychsale rang off and turned to the others. "So, that's done. But I gather you're planning to go ahead with this exorcism with or without the toy. You know, if you don't mind, I'd like to be present for this."

"Of course. You'll be an audience of one, well, two, since of course Penny will be there as well. If it goes as planned, it will all be over in a few minutes, perhaps no longer than it takes to play the song." Ringan thought for a moment. "Um—I should warn you in advance, Albert, our fiddler, Liam McCall—he's a bit of a wild man. Do you think you can cope? Because I was hoping to ask if you could provide a guest room for him, and for Matty Curran as well. He's our accordion player. We're a bit crowded for five people at Lumbe's, even without Betsy Roper's ghost popping in and out of corners."

Wychsale raised an eyebrow. "A wild man? In what way?" He saw the two women frankly grinning. "Oh, dear. I see. All right, I won't take him personally, and yes, certainly, I can offer them both beds. Now, a question. Is there anything I can do to help you prepare for this exorcism tomorrow? Anything you need in the barn itself, to facilitate things? I don't know, perhaps a portable generator, or something?"

Ringan shook his head. "This is going to be acoustic all the way. The idea is to be as true to the conditions of the time as our present surroundings will allow. I'm stopping short of trying to scare up period dress for us, because Jane and Penny tell me that Will Corby doesn't give a damn, but no electricity is to be used. And may I offer up some quiet thanks for this being June, and not January? Because I wouldn't fancy doing this on a day when darkness came early."

Penny, her arms drenched in sunlight, felt her skin crawl into gooseflesh, and the muscles of her lower back tighten. Everything suddenly seemed very close, and futile with it: tomorrow they would step into the barn, four of them with their instruments in hand, and try to summon the shade of Will Corby. There was no reason to believe the exorcism attempt would work. And even if it did succeed, there was no guarantee that Betsy, tied for so long to the cottage in which she had pumped her heart's blood away, would be able to follow . . .

"Penny." Jane, watching her, touched Penny's arm gently. "It will work. You felt it, remember? After Betsy moved through you during the storm? Do you remember how sure you were? Recapture that feeling, love. You were so certain."

"Yes." She closed her eyes and was back on the shadowy landing again, rain beating against the walls of Lumbe's as it had done for two centuries. Downstairs, a cat wailed and growled against the presence of the unearthly, and inside her own skin, the spirit of a girl done to death long before her time breathed warm, vital knowledge into her host's eyes and mind. My God, yes, it will work, she thought, and relaxed. How could I have forgotten?

The sun on her arms was warm again. She opened her eyes and smiled around the room: at Jane, watching her with a kind of fixed concentration; at Ringan, looking worried; at Wychsale, looking puzzled. "It's going to be fine," she told them. "It's going to work."

At half past five the following morning, Ringan Laine was deeply asleep. Each of the two living women at present inhabiting Lumbe's, however, was wide awake in bed.

Jane lay under a light quilt, sunlight leaking through the edges of the shuttered dormer window and onto her pillow. She had woken early, at first light, something she almost never did on the day of a live show. Music was her great love, and performance her metier; where others might go fishing or read pastoral poetry or get massaged to chase the world away, Jane sang and fluted. But today would be no ordinary performance, and the awareness of what was at stake lay below her waking mind, infecting her muscles, making her twitchy and restless.

She lay on her back, eyes closed, trying to make herself relax. After a bit, her breathing exercises began to take effect, and the tautened muscles of leg and back relaxed. The sun arced higher over the horizon, its light moving warmly, translating itself from a square of colour on her pillow to active warmth on her cheek-bones, and on the backs of her opened hands.

Yet, if her body was obedient to its relaxation training techniques, her brain was too busy for either cooperation or comfort. Something had come to her during those hypersensitive minutes before waking, on that shadowy bridge of time between surrender to night and the pull of consciousness; something, a question, a link that had struck her as vital, even in sleep. And it had slipped away with her return to the waking world.

Jane lay, breathing evenly, deliberately bringing forth what she had seen of Will Corby's life and death behind her eyelids. Obligingly, the forgotten question came back to her, fully formed, as such things do. And it was simply this: Why was Will Corby in the tithe barn at all?

With his touch on the flute she held, Jane had watched him die. Will had died with his head under water, held there until he drowned. He hadn't died in the barn. Drowning victims do not pull themselves from the site of their death, their lungs full of liquid, their chests roaring and bursting under the pressure of a medium the human body is no longer equipped to use. They don't drag themselves to the shelter of the nearest roof, at a bare minimum twenty feet away in this particular instance. They do not pick themselves up from the water and go elsewhere to die.

So why was he tied to that burned-out, ancient, oft-rebuilt structure? Was it something to do with the missing token? How had he got stuck in there, like a defaced coin dropped with casual cruelty into the gears of some universal timepiece, when he had so obviously died elsewhere? What exactly was the circumstance that held him like a spider in amber, and would not let him go?

The earth continued its eternal rotation, and the sun drew higher in the sky. Its warmth moved from Jane's cheekbone to her chin. Her mind continued its probing.

Something drew Will to that one place and shackled his spirit there. So much seemed obvious. Equally obvious was the immediate explanation of cause: Betsy. Yet something wasn't quite right there, either. It really made no sense at all. To simply say that his murdered love drew him there was a nice facile answer, if you were writing it for some overly dramatic made-for-telly movie, but in the end, the math wouldn't come out properly.

Because, when you came down to it, Betsy hadn't died in the barn, either. She herself was tied to the place in which her brother's death strike had taken the last of her heart's blood. Jane had come to understand their reactions to Betsy Roper's shade: The cold that had enveloped Ringan, that she had brought to the young Albert Wychsale more than half a century before, was the cold of her final moments of life, the stealing drowsy ice that replaces the warm lifeblood in the veins when the blood itself is lost.

Betsy's presence in Lumbe's was not only explicable; if one believed in ghosts, it was damned near inevitable. Jane's own explanation to herself about the factory girl had the ring of truth. Will Corby's presence in the tithe barn, however, was still a mystery. So Jane Castle lay in her antique bed, wondering, her mind picking at the puzzle, but finding no answers.

Across the hall, Penny lay awake, listening with mounting irritation to the irregular snores Ringan was producing. Normally, she didn't mind, or even notice; this morning, it was driving her out of her mind, as annoying as a persistent branch tapping monotonously against a window all night, just out of reach. She jerked her legs, hoping that shaking the bed might jolt him into rolling over. The effort failed. Ringan, immobile as a boulder, slumbered on.

Like Jane, Penny had woken early, and woken with the identical question in her mind. No matter how often she juggled the puzzle, one piece refused to fit the pattern: The weaver lad's presence in the old barn made no sense. She'd produced a lot of stage drama in her time, classic Greek, Jacobean, and Elizabethan. The dramatists of those periods were very fond of diving into the extremes of the human condition: the spilling of blood, violent death, the voices of the dead guiding the living toward vengeance, or making them pay. She'd done *Hamlet, Malfi,* the Scots play: these were tales about love and death, and the voices of the dead. And she could find no answer in any of them to the one question: What in sweet hell was William Corby doing in the barn, anyway? Why wasn't he off scaring the fish in the stream where he'd drowned?

As she mulled this over, Ringan let out a single, resonant plosive, a snore strong enough to stir Penny's hair. It was the final straw.

"Damnation!" she muttered, and eased herself out of bed, into her robe and slippers. Quietly, so as not to wake Jane, she slipped out of Ringan's bedroom. On the landing, she quietly closed the door and had to stifle a tiny shriek when she nearly backed into Jane, doing the same thing.

A look of wordless communication passed between them, as Ringan's snoring picked up steam and substance. Together, they went downstairs into the kitchen, in search of tea.

"You couldn't sleep, either?" Penny kept her voice soft and modulated; she was aware of a need for quiet within herself, less due to worry over waking Ringan than from some new and atavistic need to listen to the world around her. "I woke up wondering about something, and it got into my head and wouldn't get out again. Well, that, and Ringan started snoring. Bloody sinusy Scot. I seriously considered holding a pillow over his face."

"Wondering? How odd. I woke up the same way." Jane poured tea and handed Penny a cup without thinking. As she did so, her hand brushed Penny's, and her eyes went wide. With that brief physical contact, she had seen a picture in her mind's eye: a kind of tactile sense of her own question, yet seen through another's eyes.

"Oh, dear Lord." Penny's modulated speech was a raspy whisper. She held the affected hand away from her body, as if it had been scalded. "Jane? What—did you—"

"You too? Yes." Jane tried for a sip of tea. The china rattled against her teeth, and she set the saucer hastily on the table. Her own hands were shaking spasmodically. "I thought—it felt as though, I don't know—Penny? Oh God, oh sweet merciful heaven, Ringan was right. Something is happening to us. This is doing something to us. What did you see?"

"Will Corby, drowning. Not my vision, though. Yours, I take it? Water slamming into his lungs, nowhere else for it to go, bubbles on the surface and his hands thrashing, and a girl's voice screaming and a kind of gurgling—oh, *God*."

She barely reached the sink before she began to retch convulsively. Jane, afraid to offer help, unwilling to touch her for fear of setting off another of those shared scenes, stayed where she was, fighting off her own sense of vertigo.

When the sickness had passed, Penny rinsed her mouth out with cold water, and rinsed the sink clean as well. Her face had a gray, ashy tinge to it.

"All right," she said when she could finally master her own voice. Her throat felt raw, washed by acid, and her chest muscles hurt. It was, she thought, damned lucky that Jane and not she was going to have to do the singing in the coming hours. "Today really is the day, isn't it? I wonder if Betsy knows we're up to something. I wonder if this is her doing, this—this shared seeing thing we've just had."

"No clue. But I hope so. Because if not, if this is just some random coincidence in the timing, some natural progression, it very likely means that whatever's at work in this place is spinning out of any sort of control. And that would make Lumbe's unfit for living human habitation."

"It's barely fit now." Penny hated making the admission. "Why is Will Corby in the barn, Jane? By every convention of every haunting I've ever heard, he oughtn't to be anywhere near the damned place. He didn't die there. So far as any of the transcripts are concerned, he never saw the inside again after Georgie Roper went for him and dragged him out-of-doors. I don't understand. It doesn't fit. What pulls him there? And what keeps him there?"

"Your guess is as good as mine. You realise, we may never know the truth of that?" She saw the dismay in Penny's face and smiled wryly. "Maddening, isn't it?"

"That's one word for it. I just hope knowing the truth isn't a condition we have to meet for a successful exorcism. Because as pitiful as they both are, and as much sympathy as I've got for what happened to them, I'd like them gone now, and a little peace, ta ever so." Penny unlatched the top half of the kitchen door, and swung it wide. "Let's have some sun in here. Between the rain and—and everything else, I feel as though I've shut in the dark for a good long while, and I'm sick of it. Good morning, Butterball. Do you want in?"

The cat trilled, scent-marking the garden side of the door. Penny, remembering their use of Butterball as a feline dowsing rod on their first night at Lumbe's, let the lower door swing wide. Butterball strolled over the threshold as though nothing during the past two centuries had ever disturbed the cottage. Jane lifted an eyebrow.

"Well, if we're to believe this animal, there's nothing off. And frankly, I'm glad to hear it, because I really want some toast and I was getting edgy about touching anything. Visions and marmalade? No, and no. Here, Butterball, you enormous reassuring bundle of hedonism, you, here's a bit of milk, as a token of our esteem."

Penny grinned, and reached for bread. "Toast. A splendid idea. And we've got a jar of ginger preserve in the fridge. Jane, what time are Matty and Liam due here? I know Matty's got about a two-hour drive, but where is Liam coming from?"

"London, and he'd best be up and leaving just about now, because we've set this up for three this afternoon." Jane moved to the door and stared out at the tithe barn. Its wattle, daub, and ancient stone were coal-coloured, sparkling under a light coating of early morning summer dew. "I want this done with. I don't want to have to feel that they're out there, lost, unable to find each other in the dark, trapped under some sort of supernatural glass, rather like insects in a school laboratory, all pinned down." Her face was sombre, her back straight, her shoulders taut. "And it's not as though I even have to live here. Ringan's right about a few things, you know."

Jane's images were disturbing, and Penny felt a chilly cramp in the pit of her stomach. "Or like those exhibits under glass, at the Rural Life Museum. Yes. It's a bit too much, isn't it?"

"It's all of that." Jane sighed, and let her shoulders relax. "Well. If everything goes as planned, tonight will likely be the first time anyone has slept here in nearly two hundred years without wondering if the factory girl was watching from a corner somewhere."

"Do you know, I wonder if that's really true." Penny glanced around the kitchen, through the doors into the garden, and swung back around to stare into the main room. "I can't help wondering if every tenant of Lumbe's has been this receptive to them. This—this affected. I wonder if Peter Wychsale even knew they were here. How did he deal with it? He was barely ambulatory; it's not as though he could run out of doors if he got frightened."

"Is Peter the crippled ancestor who was all messed up in the Boer War, or the Crimea, or something? The one with the faithful servant who was the only one Peter would let indoors?" Penny nodded. "Right—I remember Ringan mentioning him back when he was given Lumbe's. And truth to tell, I doubt he knew Lumbe's was haunted, or cared. He must have been pretty close to a walking ghost himself. Thinking about it, he was probably so angry and bitter and resentful at the world, he'd likely have reminded Betsy too much of her brother Georgie, you know? All that rage."

"While Baby Bertie and Ringan and I, we're sympatico? Yes, I suppose so. Still, if this comes off, it won't matter anymore."

"If," Jane agreed, and the two women looked at each other, each knowing the other's thoughts, both feeling the burden of lives long gone still present somehow in the soft morning air, of unseen griefs too strong to relinquish their hold, of unwanted and unbearable memory.

A few hours later, Ringan stood alone in his tithe barn, staring at walls and floors, completely absorbed.

He had Lord Randall out of its case and propped securely in its stand, giving the grand guitar time to adjust its voice and tension to the cooler, dryer air of the barn. Ringan, meanwhile, was busily drawing mental pictures, not of passion or ghostly visitations or sudden violent death, but rather of instrument placement and the most effective acoustics to be attained under the circumstances. He had shooed the women away from the barn, with a very good argument indeed: since they both reacted to Will Corby, and he did not, it made more sense for Ringan alone to shoulder the musical setup in Will's haunted domain.

Also present in his mind, although left unvoiced, was a certain sense of unfulfilled proprietorship. After all, Lumbe's was his house and this was his barn, and except for that first day, aborted by that spine-freezing encounter on the stairs, he hadn't been presented with one chance to feel any pride of ownership.

So, standing alone in his tithe barn, Ringan hummed scales, first major, then minor, then diminished. When he found a spot in which his voice came back to him undistorted, he ran a fingernail down the guitar strings, to match the clarity. A single plangent note in the key of A curled away from Lord Randall's matchless sound box, and slipped around the barn, dying in the wrong place. With the ease of long experience, Ringan patiently moved the guitar a bare inch to the left, and then turned the stand slightly. Another hum, another pluck of Lord Randall's A string; this time, the single tone sang and rang off the ceiling, the floor, the walls, seeming to circle and meet itself in the heart of the barn. Pulling a piece of blue chalk out of one pocket, Ringan scrawled a small "R" on the floor. He had placed himself and his instrument.

That done, Ringan moved on. This time, taking the higher pitch of Jane's flute mentally into account, Ringan moved two of the hated kitchen stools he had refused to use and had left against a wall in the barn, and chalked the estimated spot with the initial "J." After a while, he had mentally placed, and subsequently marked, the best physical placement for all four members of the Broomfield Hill Quartet to what he believed would be their best acoustic advantage.

His primary task completed, Ringan stood and relaxed, letting himself really contemplate and appreciate the barn for what it was. If they could in fact rid this place of its odd tenant, he thought, it would make an excellent space in which to rehearse; it was dry, it was a perfect size for four traditional musicians to spread out comfortably, and the acoustics, while not specifically designed for live performance, nevertheless looked to work quite well in the context of rehearsals and band practice. And he doubted that even so much as the memory of Will Corby's tenure here would intrude on his life. After all, excepting only the brief surge of tenderness on that first day, he and the ghost of the weaver lad seemed to interact not at all.

This thought left an odd bitter touch at the back of Ringan's mind. The sensation was strong enough to surprise him, and that surprise demanded that he examine it. He closed his eyes, considering the question. After a few minutes of turning it over in his mind, it occurred to him that he was jealous, envious of the interaction the women were able to attain with Will Corby's spirit.

The realisation was unsettling, close to shocking. My God, Ringan thought, that's bloody petty and small. Jealousy? If ever there was a completely inappropriate reaction to not being singled out by one or the other of the spooks in this instance, jealousy would define it. Every single aspect of this haunting has been emotionally wrenching, physically debilitating, designed to give us all nightmares and force us to consider things that we'd likely rather not consider, and I'm jealous because this ghost will talk to the womenfolk and he won't give me the time of day? Am I that small a man?

The old barn offered no answers to these uncomfortable musings; it merely settled a bit more firmly on its age-blackened foundations, solid and immutable on a bed of green Somerset earth. Outside, the surrounding world was verdant and fertile, kissed by the warmth of approaching summer. All over England, fruit was ripening on the vine, tadpoles hatched and swarmed in the Carlyon, fledglings took their first tentative steps away from the safety of the nest, on the way to freedom and flight. But inside, the barn was as it had been after every fire, every rebuilding, every day and night except for that one cataclysmic event, the night of May Day in 1817.

On an impulse he could not have explained, Ringan stepped suddenly into the center of the barn.

"Will?" he said softly. "Will Corby? Are you here, weaver? Will you come out and talk to me? Will you show yourself?"

Silence hung from the packed earth to the curved oaken beams of the rafters, an untouchable and unseen curtain through which any communication seemed impossible. There was no reply, no response, only the continuing stillness.

"Come along," Ringan told the black-shadowed corners and shuttered windows. "We're coming to play you to your rest today, you and Betsy both. It's time, isn't it? You've been trapped here too long, mate. It's time you took your lady in your arms again, and got some sleep, the pair of you. This is an act of love, Will, an act of kindness. You understand kindness, I'd guess."

Something, the barest shimmer of colour, moved at the farthest edge of Ringan's peripheral vision. He jerked his head to follow, and saw nothing. Was there something, had there been something there, a speckle of prismatic light against the wall?

"We found your love gift," he said conversationally. It seemed perfectly logical to be having a one-way conversation with an empty room. It seemed fitting to acknowledge Will Corby, not only for himself, but as a man who had loved a woman. Surely, if there was to be any communication between living and dead before Will went to his rest, the shared knowledge of love would do it? "Your picture of Betsy, the one you wove for her, we found that. It's where all the world can see it, and admire your work. It's a beautiful thing, Will, almost as beautiful as Betsy was. She was a lovely, lovely girl. And I should know. She looks for all the world like my lady, and there's nothing and no one more beautiful in all creation, so far as I'm concerned."

Another shimmer, brighter than before, unmistakable this time; it was impossible to think this a mere trick of refraction and reflection. This time, Ringan had the sense to turn his head slowly, and saw the outline of something, dancing like a small square made of fireflies against the south wall of the barn. But surely this was too small to be that lovely, heart-aching bit of weaving they'd seen in the museum?

Eyes straining into the dimness, Ringan forced himself to steady and focus. What *was* that? It was certainly not cloth, not tapestry. Small, squarish, rough-hewn . . .

"Ringan?"

As Jane poked her head through the barn's door, the square of light dissolved like gelatin in water, rippled into a spattering of faint hues, and was gone. Ringan could have sworn with vexation. So close, so damnably close . . . he swallowed his exasperation and tried to sound normal.

"Yes, Jane, what's up?"

"Everyone's here. Matty arrived about ten minutes ago, and Liam got here right behind him. And Albert's just crossing the field; it looks as though he's brought something with him. Are we about ready, do you think?" Something in his stance tweaked her already heightened sense of alertness. "Ringan, did something happen? Are you all right?"

"No, I'm fine, thanks." No point in blaming Jane for an untimely interruption; the main event was just about due to begin. Nevertheless, it was frustrating. "I was just setting the marks for the best acoustics. I've done that. I'm coming out now." He followed her through the heavy doors, pausing to prop them open, and a thought occurred to him. "You said Albert's carrying something. Oh, Lord, do you suppose the fates have been merciful, and that there's any chance in hell he's somehow got hold of that bloody handloom model? Has there been any word from Dr. Wainfleet?"

"Yes, we did hear from Wainfleet and no, it's unlikely to be that loom model Albert's got, unfortunately. This is as close as I'd imagine a librarian ever gets to a weepy tantrum. Wainfleet can't find any reference anywhere to that toy loom thing. He says not only can he not pick up a trace of where it might have fetched up after the trial was done and George Roper was hanged, he can't find anything to show that it ever existed. He said he went to Street, checked various family collections, and sat up well into the small hours on the hunt. Nothing. Not a sausage. He's quite cross about it, really."

"I'm not surprised." Ringan managed a faint smile, but only for a moment. "Nothing frustrates a historian worse than being unable to prove a fact isn't really just a myth instead. I ought to know, I'm a historian myself. Penny says we're an odd, odd breed. I wonder what Albert's got, then?"

"Well, we'll know in a minute or five; he's just crossing the bridge. In the meantime, hadn't you best come talk to Matty and Liam? Penny's coping, but it's your house and your show."

"True. I'd best go take care of my hosting duties." Ringan headed up toward the cottage. "Matty! Liam! I'm damned happy to see you both. Any trouble getting down here, or finding us?"

The lawn was dotted with cars, giving it the look of a rural parking yard, at severe odds with the antiquity of the buildings forming the backdrop. Matty Curran, making happy conversation with Penny about where to find the best pastries in Denmark outside Copenhagen, lifted a hand in greeting and shook his head, smiling. His accordion case rested at his feet. "Easy drive," he said cheerfully. "Very little traffic, glorious weather, and I had good directions. No—no problems at all."

Liam, who had been standing a bit apart from the others and staring at the surrounding countryside, jerked his head toward the cottage and barn. "Nice," he said. "Very. Both yours. Is that the barn that's got the bogle in it?"

"It is, but the house has a bogle—er, ghost—as well. Lady in the cottage, name of Betsy. Gent in the barn, name of Will. Murder victims, killed by the girl's brother."

"So we're shooing them off to the Elysian Fields with a good singalong?" Ringan nodded. "Strange stuff, this is, ghosts that up and waft off toward paradise after a hey-nonny-nonny," Liam remarked. "I'm a good Catholic boy myself, and we've got a fine old raft of stuff that wants doing to put the bogles out of doors, but I never heard a good song mentioned. Who's this coming up the lane, and carrying a wee coffin? A guest for the doings?"

Ringan didn't reply at once. Wychsale had crossed the bridge, moving slowly. He was weighted down by what he held in his arms: a wooden case, thick and solid, about eighteen inches square. Liam's comment had been off the mark; the case, whatever it was, bore no resemblance whatsoever to a coffin. Ringan went to meet Wychsale.

"Hullo, Albert. Have you brought a picnic lunch?"

"Whoof." Wychsale carefully set the case down in the grass at his feet. "Hello, Ringan. Hello—I expect you're Liam McCall. You know, I really must start doing some good muscle-building exercises. A meagre little mile holding this thing, over flat ground, and look at me—red as a rose and breathing like a woman in labour. One gets out of shape before one realises, at my age."

"Well," Ringan said inanely, "it's a hot day, so heavy breathing is permitted. Good God, what am I blathering about? What have you got in the case, Albert?"

"I've got Will Corby's tapestry, is what I've got. I've got it on loan for the day. And we need to baby it, my dears, and love it, and treat it with as much care as we'd treat the Crown Jewels. I've promised the Rural Life curator."

There was a gasp from Penny, who had come up with Jane and Matty in tow. "Albert! But—but it belongs to the museum. How on earth did you get them to loan it?"

Wychsale nodded, smiling, at Matty, and shook his proferred hand. "Pleased to meet you, yes indeed, and Mr. McCall as well. How did I get them to loan it? Well. I made full use of my—what did you call it, Penny? Oh, yes—tired upper-class ancestral formality yoked about my neck by generations of mouldy old familial inheritance. In other words . . ."

"You threw your weight around and came over all baronial, and upper-crusted them into coughing it up." Penny leaned over and kissed his cheek. "Oh, Albert, I do adore you!"

Wychsale turned pink, but he was clearly pleased. "Not at all, not at all. I merely sent in one of my more formal visiting cards, the one engraved with masses of baronial arms and 'Baron Boult' and 'Right Honourable' in strategic spots. Well, all right, yes. I threw my weight around and came over all baronial and upper-crusted them halfway round the Houses of Parliament and back again. You know, if Jane wants to kiss me as well, I'd be happy to go threaten a Tory Member of Parliament for her, or some such thing. Up the revolution!"

Liam was grinning. "I like him," he told Ringan. "English aristocracy, good chap, funny. Right-minded. How mad is *that*?"

"Very, and I'm glad you like him, since you and Matty will be sleeping at the House tonight, unless you fancy a nice long drive afterward. But I'm fairly sure you won't. Albert, this is remarkable. In fact, since no one can find hide nor hair of that loom thing, this may save our exorcism for us. Can we take it out of that thing, so that it's visible? Did they give us something else to put it in, or must it stay in its case?"

"Two of my chaps are on their way over with a portable glass case. It weighed some ridiculous amount, and I was damned if I wanted to carry it. They're bringing it over, and ought to be here momentarily. Let's take this indoors. I told them to bring it to Lumbe's proper."

"Albert, no." Penny was staring at Lumbe's, her gaze fixed on the dormer windows of the upper level. "I don't think we should do that, not unless we want to risk not being able to return it to the museum in one piece at the end of the day. I have the feeling that Betsy might react to it, well, rather strongly. *Not* in the house."

"She's right." Jane's voice was flat with certainty. Matty and Liam, newcomers to the situation, glanced at each other; Liam raised one eyebrow, and Matty shrugged rather helplessly at him. "For all we know," Jane went on, "if we bring that indoors to the cottage where Betsy is, it might go up in flames. It's probably safe in the barn, I'd say, and safe enough out here. But don't bring it into Lumbe's. It might not come out again."

"As you wish." Wychsale, seeing a small estate wagon about to pull into the crowded drive, waved his arms and trotted off to meet it. A few moments later, two hefty men emerged from the wagon, opened the rear door, and carefully placed a large, glass-fronted case with a strong latch on the grass at Ringan's feet. Wychsale thanked them and waved them away. Without a word, both men climbed into the wagon and drove off.

"Ringan?"

It was Matty, emerging from a brief, quiet consultation with Liam. "Do you know, we're here; you asked us to come down and we're here, and quite glad to be here, you know. But I do think just the vestige of a clue as to *why* we're here might be in order. I take it there's been things going bump in the night? And that this is in aid of stopping the bumps? Because Jane said an exorcism, and I'd rather like to know what's what."

"Fair enough. Liam, give us an ear, mate; you'll need to hear this as well."

Having gathered their attention, Ringan explained. In concise, unemotional terms, he gave them every detail he could remember of the events of the past week, and of their own splintered reactions to the two very different revenants. He sketched in the background of the artifact they had in a wooden case at their feet, and of the artifact in whose existence they all believed, but that none of them could prove. He told them of Jane's encounter with Will Corby, of Penny's near-possession by Betsy Roper, and of the strong response evoked in both spectres by the song they had gathered to play. At the end, he looked around, meeting all their eyes in turn.

"So that's it," he said crisply. "This is how I see it happening, and I'd be grateful if anyone sees a flaw in this scenario, or has a better idea. We bring what we've got—tapestry, glass case, instruments, and ourselves—into the barn, and close the doors—this is strictly a private party. We set up the glass case with the tapestry; it ought to be an awfully strong pull for Will Corby, not that he's shown he needs any more reasons to hang about in the barn than he's already got. We set ourselves up, and I've already done the acoustics; you'll find everything marked out, but feel free to move it around if you like a different spot better. There's one spot that's off-limits, though, halfway along the base of the south wall. There's a straw bed, or was once, and if you stand there, you might just get Will Corby materialising in your knickers. We'll put the tapestry there, case and all. It makes sense to me."

"Ringan—what about us?" Penny asked. "Is there anything Albert and I ought to be doing?"

"Nothing that I can think of. But," Ringan added with mordant humour, "that doesn't mean our residents won't have a few notions of their own about what you ought to be doing."

Penny glanced at Albert, and nodded. She had gone very pale. Ringan's meaning was clear: It was highly possible that should the psychic drag of the music and the talisman together prove a potent enough combination to pull Betsy Roper from her limbo indoors at Lumbe's to here where her lover waited in the barn, she might very well come straight through Penny to do it.

"Right. Albert, Penny, we need to bring the tapestry and the glass case into the barn. And if everyone's ready, let's get this show started," Ringan said, and stepped toward the barn.

Nine

Where are the girls, I will tell you plain
The girls have gone to weave by steam
And if you'd find them, you must rise at dawn
And trudge to the mill in the early morn.

"What a weird room this is."

The words were distorted. Liam, his fiddle jammed under chin as he prepared to tune it, spoke with the instrument's bridge pressed up against his tonsils.

"It is, rather. I've never been inside anything quite like this." Matty, as placid as ever, had unhooked his concertina and opened it, leaving the larger accordion—he'd brought both along—against the wall, just inside the barn's doors. He played a few notes on the squeezebox, letting them pipe out into the still air. They sounded merry, and incongruously bright. "The proportions, I mean; didn't you say this was supposed to be a tithe barn? I'm not sure just what Liam was meaning."

"Liam was meaning that it's a weird room." The Irishman rubbed rosin on his bowstrings with gusto. "Liam was meaning that he'd not die of shock to see Count Dracula fly out from behind one of those big roof beams, bite a few jugulars, laugh in our faces, and flap away toward the Continent where they keep his castle." He pulled the bow across the strings, and the notes spun skyward, bounced off the roof, and died gracefully into a deep, harmonious hum. "When I say weird, mate, that's just what I mean. A weird, weird room. Nice acoustics, though."

"Definitely nice acoustics, at least for my flute. Let's see how it does with vocalising." Jane opened her flute case, exposing the vintage silver instrument on its bed of worn gold velvet. That done, she took a sip from the water bottle she always carried, and flexed her voice, letting fly with a beautiful vocal scale.

Wychsale, who'd been watching the musical preparations around him with deep interest, jumped and nearly pulled a muscle in his neck twisting his head around. Jane's singing voice was always lovely. In this space, enclosed by stone and cob, directed in and out of vagrant corners by the directional changes made unavoidable by the presence of those big roof beams, the sheer power and clarity of Jane's voice had an unearthly quality to it. It did odd things to the nervous system.

Wychsale felt a little tremor move down the length of his spine, a frisson of something he would later identify as an uncomfortably close brush with the possibility of the eternal verities. Where would they go, those two dead children, once the song was over and done? Here in the waking world of the modern age, these people would pack up their instruments and react to whatever was to happen today. They would exclaim, discuss, remember; they would drink tea and cider and eat their dinner. Their lives would go on, until their moment came to move on, as such a moment comes to everyone in the end.

But Will Corby, Betsy Roper, where would they be? The result of this thing the living were planning to do, would it free the dead, or simply cast them out into some unimaginable state of nonexistence? And if the final destination was, in fact, nowhere—nothingness, an impossible void—then was this, in fact, an act of evil? How was it possible for the human mind and heart to understand such questions, much less answer them?

To Albert Wychsale, raised in the comfortable bosom of the Anglican church, these were questions he had never been encouraged to ask. He was conscious of a deep discomfort, and for the first time, he allowed himself to fully remember those long-ago moments on the cottage stairs, and to understand the weight of what they hoped to accomplish with this performance.

"Albert, would you and Penny set up the tapestry in its glass case?" Ringan picked up Lord Randall and slung the leather strap over his shoulder. In his arms, the instrument looked imposing; Ringan was neither overly tall nor especially broad, and a Martin D-45 is a very large guitar. "Penny and Jane know where it ought to go; they're the ones who had to tell me."

For Albert Wychsale, the events of the day were taking on a strange cast. He found himself disinclined to speak aloud; there was a sense of purpose that hung palpably in the cool air, something against which the sound of his own voice would seem small, insignificant, perhaps even disruptive. He looked mutely at Penny and saw his own feelings reflected in her face.

In silence, he knelt and opened the wooden carrying case in which Will Corby's tapestry lay. It had been carefully folded, with sheets of acid-free paper placed between every layer, as well as above and beneath.

Still in silence, Wychsale and Penny carried the heavy glass case to the barn's south wall. They found the four latches, opened it; together, they laid acid-free paper at the bottom. Carefully, gently, they unfolded the tapestry and opened it out, holding it in the air between them, displaying it for a moment to the band, and to whoever else might be watching, unseen and unacknowledged.

Not a word had been spoken. For a few more moments, silence draped the barn like a funerary shroud. Into that absolute quiet came the voice of the stream.

To Penny, holding her two fragile woven corners, it was the loudest sound she had ever heard. The voice of the water that had poured into Will Corby's lungs filled the room with the roar of a tsunami, crashing into flesh, wood, and stone with a force so relentless, it was nearly tangible. It thundered like a cavalry of a thousand mounted horsemen, shaking the building.

For just a moment, Penny wondered if she alone was hearing it. She made herself look at the others—at Ringan, grim-faced and tense; at Matty, wide-eyed with disbelief; at Liam, elongated and pugnacious, his waist-length hair seeming to crackle with expectation. Their faces told her nothing; they might well have been painted figures, so unrevealing were they. Then she met Jane's eyes, and knew she was not alone in what she was experiencing. The voice of the stream was back in the barn, and who only knew if, even with the power of the full band behind them, they were going to be able to drown it out . . .

"Quickly." Wychsale was whispering, as if he understood that this was the only way to cut through the power and density of that unnatural barrage. "Hurry. We have to get this thing under glass, and we have to do it now. Penny—please. Help me!"

She heard horror, and urgency. Around her, strange things were beginning to happen to the shapes, to the very fabric, of the barn's interior. Joiner's lines between the planks and boards, cut and sealed to be straight, seemed to waver in crazy serpentine patterns. Penny saw a splash of colour, moving like the beam of a torch along the topmost edge of the walls where they met the ceiling. The atmosphere, with the passing of each moment, was thickening around them. And what was she hearing—was that voices, human voices, beneath the cacophony that was the angry invisible water raging through their world . . . ?

"Penny!"

She jerked her head back to Wychsale, and saw the naked terror in his face. His fear brought her back to herself; she went down to a knee and, with shaking hands that seemed numb and disconnected from her body and brain, fumbled her half of the tapestry into its glass case. They smoothed it flat, a chore that, to Penny's disarranged senses, seemed to take an eternity. Together, she and Wychsale snapped the glass lid down and pushed the fasteners closed.

"Come along," Wychsale told her thinly. "Move away. This— this isn't a safe place." He caught at her hand and pulled her toward the doors.

What are they waiting for, Penny wondered, why don't they play? If they don't start soon, the stream will take us all. It must be about to come through the doors, the windows. The stream—it must have burst its banks. It's coming in. It couldn't be this loud if it wasn't about to—

"On three," Ringan shouted, "one—two—*three!*" and Penny

screamed, a tiny whistling scratch that she swallowed at once. Wychsale had her by the hand, his fingers laced hard through hers. She was completely unaware of his touch. All of her conscious mind was directed against the barrage of watery noise.

For Broomfield Hill, a professional band comprised of four professional musicians, the song started off raggedly, slightly out of sync. Matty, his eyes half-closed with the same pain that was battering at Penny's senses, came in a quick half beat later than Ringan and Liam, and faltered as he tried to adjust. Jane, whose teeth were chattering, was having some difficulty handling her flute; she managed to play the melody line that was traditional for her instrument, but the pitch, for the first bars, was ragged, and the volume uneven. Ringan and Liam, both steady, held the pace and timing in place.

Ringan waited for Jane to finish the piping run that signals the song's transition from introductory notes to sung verse. She turned her head, saw his nod, and began the first verse.

"I am a hand-weaver to my trade, I fell in love with a factory maid, and if I could but her favour win, I'd stand beside her and weave by steam."

The howl of the water, gurgling and roaring, began a subtle shift downward. There was a momentary pause, a lessening of intensity. They all felt it. They all heard it.

Ringan came in, singing the second verse with Jane, their voices soaring together in a clean line of storytelling.

"My father to me scornful said, how could you fancy a factory maid? When you could have girls fine and gay, dressed like unto the Queen of May?"

Light, a visual impossibility that was icy dots of colour, came through the shutters. The same light came through the floor. Something under the barn, and something outside and around it, bled out in a pure cold flood of prismatic brilliance. It leaked through the shutter slats and welled up from the heart of the earth below them, trickling and spreading like chilly lava, around the glass case where the tapestry rested.

"Ringan? There's something—I don't . . ." Matty faltered, his hands slowing on the concertina.

"For God's sake, don't stop. Keep playing!" Ringan watched the floor beneath the case. Something else was coming, born of the chill and unnatural light that flashed and pulsed around them; something the women had seen before, the outlines of a pile of sacks. Its edges grew rapidly more distinct, its shape more defined. It solidified and firmed itself, curling its corners beneath the tapestry, nesting it.

"As for your fine girls, I don't care, if I could but enjoy my dear, I'd stand in the factory all the day, and she and I'd keep our shuttles in play."

With no warning and without visible effort, Will Corby was there. They all saw him this time, Ringan, Wychsale, everyone in the barn. Later, none of them would agree on where he had come from; it seemed to each of them as though he had first manifested from a different angle, a different corner, a different source. Still, wherever he had come from, here he was, the visible shade of a boy done to death in a different place, a different time.

He held the carved token, of which no trace had been found. He cradled it, smoothed it, touched it; he rolled it between his broad, well-kept fingers. They all saw it, and Ringan, his own fingers manipulating the frets and strings of Lord Randall, made a mental note to offer Penny a handsome apology. He could see it quite clearly, and she'd been right all along. It was a toy or model of a handloom, smaller somehow than he had mentally envisioned it, no more than six inches in diameter. No wonder it was lost, he thought, a thing as tiny as that.

"Something's happening over there." It was Liam, staring in fascination but completely unfazed, his wildly sawing bow never missing the perfect point on the fiddle's strings. "Look. You've got one bogle, and another bogle coming in."

Penny knew that Betsy was coming before anyone else saw her. She felt her there, felt the struggle inside her own bones, first warm, then the never-to-be-forgotten touch of death's dark potency slowing the blood in her veins. For a brief moment, a moment that lasted as long as the eternity for which Betsy had been caught in those last moments of her own life, Penny saw the room through Betsy's eyes.

She saw misty shapes, shadows perhaps, or even things out of her imagination. None of them were real, none of them living people, none of them of any importance to her. Waxworks, or shadows, that's what they were. She didn't know what they were doing, and it didn't matter. All that mattered was Will, Will come to meet her as he always had and always would, Will spreading the marvellous thing he'd woven for her, strand by strand of rough-dyed yarn, done on the quiet when his father might not see or know what his only son was doing on the family's loom at the bottom of the Corbys' garden. Most of all, Will spreading it across the rough bed that was, to her, as fine as any goose-feather, silk-covered place where the King himself might lay him down to rest.

"I went to my love's bedroom door where often times I had been before, but I could not speak, nor yet get in the pleasant bed that my love lies in . . ."

And Will, he had her gift, hard by him. She'd kept two precious coins from her factory wages aside, and paid the old market gardener over to Yatton to carve him that little loom. He could read, the old man; he'd carved a letter E, for Elizabeth, right there into the bottom of it. He'd shown her, and she'd traced it with her finger, trying to commit the shape of a letter she couldn't read to her memory: E for Elizabeth, who gives this token of her love to you. A special night this was, a fine night, with illuminations and dancing and each with a token of their love to give the other, with only love to come. She'd have to find a place to keep her gift; maybe right here in the barn, folded small, hidden away. It wouldn't do to have it where anyone might find it.

Penny stood and stared, a tender smile that was never her own curving her lips into sensuality. Betsy moved out of her and away from her, passed through and beyond, and came to rest on the bed of sacks with its bright blanket, touching the image of herself with wonder and delight.

"Oh, God," Ringan whispered. He had seen Penny's face, and he knew what had happened. There was no way to gauge the effects of Betsy's tiny pause in vital flesh not her own. The song, blessedly, was at an instrumental section, without lyric; he could not have sung had his life depended on it. Nor did he dare stop play-ing; to stop now might do immeasurable harm.

Ringan glanced at Wychsale, who had been holding Penny's hand throughout. He willed him with a silent, inchoate prayer: please, Ringan begged in his mind to whoever might be listening, please, get the Right Hon to turn around, to look at Penny. Read my mind, he begged. Come on, mate, read it and see how badly I need you to do this. Tell me she's still here. Please.

Wychsale made no move. But Penny stood, still and straight, and her mouth began to slacken. In no longer than it took for the musicians to play one line of instrumental music, her face had cleared and she was Penny again. Ringan, slumped with unspeak-able relief, played on, drawing breath to sing.

There was something in her eyes now, sorrow and pity and an awareness that held wonder. Her gaze never left the pair on the bed of sacks.

"How can you say it's a pleasant bed when none lies there but a factory maid? Oh, a factory lass although she be, blessed is the man who would enjoy she . . ."

The lovers spoke.

Wychsale, his nervous system still jangling and shocked from the touch of the moving dead against him, heard Will Corby's voice. He heard Betsy reply. They were voices only, tones, shades of amusement and pleasure and reaction; he could distinguish no individual words. But that he was hearing the hearts and minds of these children, he had no doubt.

And they really were children. It came to him, as life returned to the hand that had brushed Betsy Roper on her passage toward her final earthly destination, how very young these two had been.

Betsy put her arms up, and laced them around Will's neck, pulling his face down to her own. Although the gesture was beyond tender, it was not a kiss; she seemed to be whispering to him. As if in response, he turned the little wooden toy upside down. The watchers saw her point to something, saw her reach a small calloused finger out to touch it, saw the curving courtesan's smile light her face. For just a second, the translucency that marked her seemed to solidify, melding into living flesh.

"E is for Elizabeth, you know." Penny's voice was not loud, but it rang across the room. It was only then that everyone realised that the howl of the water had dropped; it was still there, still audible, but it dropped back to the volume level at which Penny and Jane had first heard it.

"What's she on about, then?" Liam muttered, but no one heard him over the swell of the music, the glide of invisible water, the murmer of wordless, impossible voices that came from everywhere and nowhere.

Wychsale suddenly reached out and took Penny's hand again. She made no objection; he wasn't even sure she noticed.

"It's the carver's mark," she remarked dreamily. "You know, the old man who made it. He marked it with an E. That's for Elizabeth. But she can't read, Elizabeth can't. Still, she's proud it's there, and Will can read it for her. The letter E, for Elizabeth. Because that's her name."

Betsy kissed him, a deep kiss, and Will slipped one hand down to the small of her back. It was a gesture of extreme ease and familiarity. Wychsale, feeling the passion mounting and beginning its play, let go of Penny's hand again. He felt, obscurely, as if he had been unfairly caught in a situation that made him watch something that was not at all his affair. The sense of voyeurism was unsettling, and inherently distasteful.

"A pleasant thought's come to me mind as I turned down the sheets so fine and saw her two breasts standing so like two white hills all covered with snow . . ."

The girl lay back on the cloth that bore her woven image. Her eyes had colour now, and depth; they could all see the stormy gray, ringed with a shimmery line of smoky gold. Will put his hands around that tiny waist, slid them up, found the bodice. One hand traced the shape of her breasts, and slid up to touch her lips. Betsy pulled him down to her, this time in a kiss. Unnervingly, her features seemed to run into his, coming together like paint on a fresco, damaged by the rain. Around them, the unnatural light swelled and flickered.

Jane was the first to see what was happening, what was about to happen: the third presence pouring into their reality. It was more primal feeling than recognisable figure, moving from one world to another with no warning, there in a heartbeat. He brought violence with him, a bitter relentless thing that filled the barn. It enveloped the two on the bed like the wings of some dark bird beating above them. And the voice of the water came crashing back, brutal, not to be borne, too loud and too heavy for the human spirit to withstand.

The two on the bed made of sacks were pulled viciously apart. Betsy rolled off, the tapestry coming free with her, clutched in a grip as tight as any rigor. Will had lost sight of her; the raw violent darkness was between them and it was plain that Will, not Betsy, was the object of its rage.

"So strong," Penny whispered, "too strong. Oh please, no."

It pulled Will Corby halfway up from where he lay. Will came up, obviously confused and unsure as to the source of the attack, unable to see Betsy.

Betsy grabbed at the interloper. With her one free hand, she caught him by the hair and tried to wrench him back and away from Will. If any of the three in this tableau spoke, or cried out, no sounds were audible to those who watched from the present day: the universe had contracted to water and song.

"The loom goes click and the loom goes clack, the shuttle flies forward and then flies back; the weaver's so bent that he's like to crack—such a wearisome trade is the weaver."

Lightning streaked inside that vortex of furious darkness. It flashed out, smoking through the air, a bright blade of something without a name, but with one purpose only, to wound. It came down, striking out, finding a target. Everything seemed to stop, held in time and place, forced into immobility by the sheer weight of surprise.

For a heartbeat, the light-limned shape that had been Betsy Roper stood as she had been. From her left hand dangled the heavy

174

cloth weaving. Then her right hand moved, in a slow gesture of infinite pain, and disbelief. It came up to where the blow had landed, touching, searching there until it found the spot, knowing and accepting that this strike had been mortal.

She turned away, her knees collapsing beneath her, and was gone. It was too fast for living eyes to follow, too unexpected to stop; a moment, only a moment, and the shape of a girl became a fractured outline, a travesty of human form. Then she was nothing at all, no more than a poignant memory.

"Where are the girls, I will tell you plain: The girls have gone to weave by steam. And if you'd find them, you must rise at dawn and trudge to the mill in the early morn."

Will Corby gave up. This, they could all see happen: only Penny, her eyes blinded by the tears of Betsy Roper's passing, could spare nothing of herself to watch. But Will had seen the blow, and understood that Betsy was gone, lost to him. At that moment, he stopped struggling.

Water filled the barn, invisible but potent. This time, it was more than sound; the reality of water was with them, pouring into their lungs, stinging their eyes, bearing them away. Someone shouted, it might have been Liam or Matty; they were choking, all of them, drowning, struggling for air and breath. The sack bed and the weaver's shade were invisible now, the life gone out, welcoming death and obscured by the cloud of violence and murder that had come so suddenly and caused such pain and such damage.

The sound of the water, the undefined yet undeniable sense of it, was the first thing to go. It reached a crescendo, deafening and relentless, and was gone. No more than a second, and the barn was clear of it.

The frozen rainbows of light pulsed once, solar flares beyond human understanding, and turned to clear cool air. The bed went next into the ether, leaving behind no trace of itself. The glass case that had held and protected Will Corby's token throughout the proceedings sat solidly on the floor where the light and the bed had been, where two lovers had laughed and touched and turned to see their own deaths coming to them.

The music ran through two repetitions of the main melody line, a charming four-part harmonic of flute, guitar, fiddle, concertina. It held for the requisite two beats, struck the ultimate note, and stopped. Four musicians and two members of the audience stood in a quiet barn. There were no ghosts, no unpleasant echoes; no drama. The barn was just a cool dry room, disturbed by nothing more than the sound of their breathing and the memory of musical notes in the air.

Broomfield Hill had finished their song.

"Did it really happen?"

Jane, cross-legged on the floor of Lumbe's main room, put the question. Dusk had just completed its slow slide into night. Out-of-doors, the birds whose domain were the sunlit hours had stopped calling and gone to roost. Insects moved out in their quest for sustenance only to become sustenance themselves, as bats echolocated, attacking and feeding with a near-silent rush of wings. In gardens all over the southern counties, flowers that hid from the day opened themselves to the night sky: moonflower, evening primrose, angel's trumpet.

Liam and Matty had gone back to the manor house with Wychsale, after he had promised them both a superb dinner and as much cider as they could hold. Matty had to get home for a family outing the next day, and would need an early start. Liam and Wychsale, who had been locked in an animated argument about the logistics of illegal liquor manufacturing when they left, were showing signs of becoming the oddest of inseparable cronies.

"It happened." Ringan studied his empty plate. Surrounding them were cartons of takeout food, depleted now of their weight of *chana masala* and prawn vindaloo and folded *naan* bread. The afternoon's ordeal in the barn had left them ravenously hungry; none of them could remember a time when so much food had been required, simply to stoke their own belief that they, themselves, were still breathing and moving. It was as if, during those few minutes of song, they had burned off all their existing reserves of energy, and left the batteries dry. "It not only happened, it did what it was supposed to do. We're clear now. Honestly, can't you feel it?"

Jane nodded in silence. No reply was needed; the question was rhetorical. The certainty that Will and Betsy had gone was beyond question. All of them, even the two who had come into the day's proceedings with no prior knowledge of what Lumbe's normal state should be, could feel the difference.

"There are so many things we're never going to know." Penny lay on her back, staring up at the ceiling; Ringan, unwilling to relinquish physical contact in the hours after their return to the cottage, had finally been persuaded to let go of her hand. He had required almost as much reassurance that she was truly the woman he knew as he had required food and conversation, for comfort's sake. "But at least one of the big questions was answered, the one that was pinching at me the most. I know it was worrying Jane, as well. I know why Will couldn't let go of his ties to the barn."

"He did die there." Jane closed her eyes, remembering her brief contact with the boy in the barn, his slow movements, his bumpy broken nose, the weight of his sorrow. He had left something of himself with her, even as some part of Betsy Roper would always remain with Penny. "He saw George stab Betsy, when she tried to pull George off him, and he knew it was fatal. He gave up then. He accepted his own death, there in the barn."

"He let Georgie kill him. Christ, the poor sod. No reason to live, no desire to stay with Betsy gone. So yes, in the truest sense of the word, he really did die in the barn, even if his heart stopped down at the stream. It's just semantics, really." Ringan reached for a plastic container, found a few shreds of chicken, picked them out with his fingers, and swallowed them whole. "Why do you suppose Betsy was all over the house? On the stairs, in the best bedroom?"

"Well—she lived here, didn't she?" Jane sounded mellow. "I mean, she didn't just die here, she was born here. And she never left. Why would Will feel that way about the barn? He wouldn't."

"True. Seventeen years of her life spent right here. Considering her life, though, I'd have thought she'd be glad to be done with this place." He was quiet a moment and then remarked, with seeming irrelevance, "There's something life-affirming about eating, isn't there?"

"Indeed. You know, in *Dracula,* Bram Stoker had Renfield saying that the blood was the life, but for me, I'd have to go with chocolate, or possibly a good thick centre-cut chop and two veg on the side. Or even a three-egg omelette with rather a lot of cheese melted in." Penny, in the act of rolling over and sitting up, heard a thump in the kitchen and caught her breath. Then she heard a trill, remembered that they'd left the Dutch door latched open, and laughed. "Butterball! Here, silly puss, come along."

The cat trotted in, trailing his tail like a banner, his whiskers at attention, scenting for food. He caught the smell of Indian spices, wrinkled his nose, and curled up beside Jane.

"It's a lucky thing that the glass case held up." Ringan had closed his eyes. He was drowsy with dinner, with the events of the day, but he was also aware of a deep satisfaction. The two who had lingered were free, and for the first time, he felt that Lumbe's had become entirely his own. "I wouldn't have wanted to be Albert had anything nasty happened to that tapestry, baron or no baron. Can you imagine trying to explain what happened today to a nice pedantic museum curator? 'Sorry, mate, we were sending a pair of ghosts off to their eternal rest, and I'm afraid your priceless bit of history was part of the cost of admission.'"

Penny was quiet. The smaller things had been clarified, it was true, but the great question remained, and would always remain. It had been the driving force behind human history, that question; it had led to the founding of religions and the crafting of gods, to brutality and greatness of heart and the evolution of that most definitive of human traits, conscience.

Where had they gone, those two? Penny, a modern woman who who made her living by practicing the traditions and conventions of language and drama, knew that there ought to be written words and scenes for what they had undergone and caused to happen this day. But for Betsy Roper and Will Corby, dying to music and sent away to some unimaginable place, what words would suffice, and who had written those words? Where had they gone? Nothing seemed appropriate, somehow . . .

" 'To be imprison'd in the viewless winds,' " she said softly. The quotation had come whole into her head, as if sitting in her subconscious, awaiting its cue to emerge. " 'And blown with restless violence round about the pendant world.' "

The room was silent as the others considered. Ringan edged closer and put his arm around her shoulders. She sighed, a long release of pent-up tension. It had been a very long day.

"Was that Shakespeare?" Jane was gently stroking Butterball; they all seemed to need the reassurance of touch tonight.

"*Measure for Measure*. That's actually the last bit of the quotation, now I think of it. The rest of it, the opening lines that lead into it, well—"

"Go on, tell us." Ringan's arm was comforting around her. "The questions that came up today are mostly too big for me to want to look at properly. So I'm always glad for Shakespeare, what with his useful little knack for the appropriate language. What does he say, love?"

Penny closed her eyes, thought, and found the entire quote in her mind. " 'Ay, but to die and go we know not where; to lie in cold obstruction and to rot; this sensible warm motion to become a kneaded clod; and the delighted spirit to bathe in fiery floods, or to reside in thrilling regions of deep-ribbed ice.' Then it follows on with that bit about the viewless winds." She rubbed her face against Ringan's shoulder. "Crikey. And now for a few words from our sponsor. He really does have something for everything, doesn't he?"

"Not everything," Jane said quietly. "Do you know, this is awfully small, but I have a confession to make. It's going to drive me a bit batty from now until I hit the viewless winds myself, not knowing what happened to that damned wooden loom."

Epilogue

At eight o'clock on an early June morning in 1817, a boy called George Roper stood at the foot of a scaffold, awaiting his date with the hangman in accordance with the decision imposed by His Majesty's decree.

His hands tied behind his back, he watched through eyes that were too frightened and too numb to feel or understand as the hangman, his own features obscured by a black hood, pulled a white hood out and offered it wordlessly to George. The hangman, who when he was not supplementing his income in this fashion, was in fact a middle-aged man with three children and a faltering business weaving seaworthy rope for a coast chandlery. He had served as hangman many times before, and he was experienced enough in the ways of those about to die to know that the boy's lack of response was indicative of nothing more than incomprehension. The lad was past all earthly will or desire, and if he was not, his luck was surely out, since the choice of whether or not to meet the eyes of his fellows as the drop fell open and his neck broke was the only choice he still had coming in this life.

It was the hangman's custom to take a lack of response as an affirmative; mostly those about to swing were too far gone in fear to answer, leaving the choice up to him. He fitted the white hood over George Roper's head, pulling the drawstring just snug enough to hold it in place. It would not interfere with the action of the noose; its only purpose was an intended kindness, keeping the condemned man from the horror of seeing his own terror reflected in the eyes of those who had come to watch him pay for his crime.

The hangman nodded at the constable, who was holding George Roper's arm. George stumbled a bit, walking up the tilted plank; many hangmen would have chosen to wait until his subject stood directly beneath the sturdy oak arm from which the noose depended before fitting that blinding hood. This particular hangman, however, was kindly enough at heart. Even if he did have a duty and a responsibility to carry out the direst extreme of His Majesty's law, he did whatever he felt might make the end a bit easier. He'd always figured it must be a bad thing indeed to meet those watching eyes, some mean, some pitying. At least none of the boy's family had come to watch. Likely they couldn't bear it, however they felt toward their son; thanks to him, they'd already lost a beloved daughter.

The constable walked George Roper to the chalked mark below the noose, and formally handed his charge to the hangman. The hangman, setting the noose around George's neck and tightening it with the ease of long practise, took a moment to glance up at the sky. There looked to be rain coming; black clouds had formed off around Glastonbury Tor, looking weirdly like the wings of some enormous crow made of dark water.

A rumble of thunder boomed and spoke across the town square. It was a right peculiar thing, the hangman thought, but sometimes it seemed to him that every time he presided over a hanging in Glastonbury, one of these storms would come through, soaking the land, showing God's creation in its noisiest, angriest light.

The attending sexton read a passage from the Bible. He asked for the Lord's mercy on George Roper's soul. The hangman pulled the lever, and the trap beneath George Roper's feet opened. He had gone to keep his own appointment with the viewless winds.

Between Glastonbury and Street, in a tithe barn that was larger than it would be nearly two centuries later, a small wooden toy lay forgotten against the south wall. Since the man for whom it had been made had felt his lungs burst in the stream that ran beside this old barn, the toy had lain where it had fallen. There was a small smear of dried blood on it, an ugly rusty colour. A larger smear streaked the floor beside it.

It was eight o'clock in the morning precisely. The barn, in the direct shadow of Glastonbury Tor, was uninhabited and locked.

The first bolt of lightning struck the stones on the south wall at the first stroke of eight. In Glastonbury, the sexton had just closed his Bible, and the hangman reached for the release lever. On the floor of the barn, where earth met stone and where Will Corby's *memento mori* lay, the packed earth glowed briefly scarlet. A wisp of smoke curled up from the wooden toy.

Thunder crashed, booming through the ruined towers of Glastonbury Abbey, making the branches of Joseph of Arimathea's thorn tree dance briefly. The second stroke of lightning, on a straight line from the black clouds above the Tor, ignited the south wall of the barn. It began to burn quickly, the flames taking on the old wood, greedy and hungry, filling the barn with smoke. Inside, the wooden toy was already a charred pile of ash.

In Glastonbury, George Roper's feet had stopped kicking. They dangled, still and lifeless, looking incongruous and surreal through the scaffold's trapdoor.

It would be some time before the Wychsale farm workers noticed the smoke over the old tithe barn. They would come across the small stone bridge, buckets in hand, taking water from the stream, forming a living line so that they might put the fire out before it spread. In fact, the fire itself would have gone out before they got there; it had come for a particular purpose and, its appetite sated, it allowed itself to die.

The barn had burned before, and it would surely burn again. In the meantime, it would be rebuilt, smaller than ever. And life in the countryside would go on as before.